"I should like to understand, Richard."

As Elizabeth spoke, she longed to brush the hair back from Richard's brow and hold him close.

"You are the most remarkable girl," he told her. And neither noticed that somehow her hand was in his. Richard began quietly to tell her his story.

Elizabeth admired Richard for his bravery, handsome bearing and easy address, but her heart became completely engaged by this glimpse of an endearing little boy who had been so cruelly hurt.

"You do understand, Elizabeth? My first priority must be to regain the estate, and set my affairs in order. It's a vow I made long ago, and until I've done that and taken my rightful place, I dare not speak what's in my heart."

Elizabeth could not resist a gentle tease. "Do you fear you'll change your mind?"

He reached up to caress a delicate cheek. "No fear of that. I think it was destined long ago. Only look how my heart led me here when I'd no intention of seeing you."

"Then trust your heart," she said softly.

Books by Jeanne Carmichael

HARLEQUIN REGENCY ROMANCE
56–A TOUCH OF BLACKMAIL

QUEST FOR VENGEANCE

JEANNE CARMICHAEL

Harlequin Books

TORONTO • NEW YORK • LONDON
AMSTERDAM • PARIS • SYDNEY • HAMBURG
STOCKHOLM • ATHENS • TOKYO • MILAN
MADRID • WARSAW • BUDAPEST • AUCKLAND

For Rose,
whom I consider the embodiment of a true lady,
and who has earned not only my love,
but my respect

Published February 1992

ISBN 0-373-31167-2

QUEST FOR VENGEANCE

CHAPTER ONE

RICHARD ST. SYMINGTON-DANVERS made one final adjustment to his neckcloth, rose and turned to his valet. "Well, what say you, Roscoe? Do I look a proper Englishman?"

The wiry little Italian assisting him looked up and down his master's long frame. Curling brown locks were brushed stylishly to fall across the wide brow. His neckcloth was tied to a nicety that would have found approval with Beau Brummel himself, and the deep blue jacket had been designed by Weston especially to accommodate Richard's broad shoulders. Buff pantaloons moulded long legs which had no need of padding, and glossy black boots by Hoby proclaimed him every inch the gentleman. Only the crescent-shaped scar below the right eye gave one pause. It stood out, startlingly white against Richard's deeply bronzed skin which made his pale blue eyes look cold, and marked him as more than the usual London dandy.

"What ails you, man? You've never been reluctant to express your opinion before."

"You look better 'an most, as my lord well knows—"

"Quiet! Or do you wish to completely undo me?"

Roscoe lowered his voice to a whisper. "I've been calling you *my* lord for the better part of six years. It's right hard not to all of a sudden." He turned away, mumbling beneath his breath.

Richard grinned at him. "Yes, I know. And I know you and Kirby disapprove, but it's only for a time. Besides, it's not as though I were plain Mr. Danvers passing myself off as a lord. If that were the case, you might have cause to complain."

"Aye, but them belowstairs thinks as how they're better 'an us. They'd show a different face if they was to know who you really are. And old Josiah Danvers wouldn't be approving, either. If he knows what you're up to, he must be turning in his grave."

"Roscoe, we've covered this ground a hundred times. If I'm ever to recover what's rightfully mine, I can't appear as St. Symington yet."

"Supposing someone recognizes you? What then, *Mr.* Danvers?"

"It's hardly likely, since I've not set foot in England for sixteen years. Don't forget I was only ten when I left. And even you must admit I've changed more than a little."

Roscoe gave a bark of laughter. "It's a point. A sorrier, skinnier waif than you was when I first laid eyes on you, I never seen. And look at ye now. It's a grand job I've done, no doubt. There's not many an Englishman could fill out that jacket the way you do." He reached up a possessive hand and whisked away an imaginary piece of lint.

Richard ignored him, picking up a large diamond ring. He tried it on his shapely finger. "Too much, do you think?"

"Not if you is wishful of impressing 'em with your wealth."

Reluctantly, he removed the ring. "No, I can't risk appearing ostentatious. I think I'd be better off to seem rather unassuming. The English seem to count that as a virtue."

"The English! Don't be forgetting you're English, too, my—*Mr. Danvers,* for all your years in India. Remarks like that won't endear you."

"No, and neither will being late. I'm told Lady Castlereigh is a stickler for punctuality. Tell Kirby to bring round the carriage."

Roscoe went ahead, and after a few minutes, Richard followed. He strolled down the broad staircase of the townhouse he was leasing. There was no one about in the hall, and mindful of Roscoe's words, he jerked the bellcord. It was several minutes before the butler appeared.

"You rang, Mr. Danvers?" the man asked, voice and manner designed to convey how inappropriate he found Richard's behaviour.

Richard studied his butler, a pompous older man, nearly bald and puffed up with his own consequence. He grew nervous under Richard's unrelenting stare, and began to fidget.

"Philbin, is it? I am going out, Philbin, and when I return I shall expect either you or a footman to open the door at once. In the future I expect someone in attendance at all times. If you cannot manage the staff efficiently, I shall find someone who can. Do we understand each other?" Richard's voice was soft, without the slightest hint of anger or unpleasantness. But Philbin, looking into the cold blue eyes, had little doubt that Richard Danvers meant exactly what he said.

"Yes, Mr. Danvers. Of course, sir. I'm very sorry, sir. I assure you it won't happen again."

"Thank you, Philbin. I feel certain I can rely on you."

Roscoe opened the door and was unable to hide his surprise at seeing the ubiquitous Philbin fawning over

Richard. His master winked as the butler helped him on with his cape and handed him his gloves. Richard strolled out as though he hadn't a care in the world.

Kirby had the carriage waiting, and it was apparent from his sour countenance that he and Roscoe had been discussing what they termed "Richard's obsession." They both thought him run mad. Richard settled himself without a word, and gave him the nod to start.

It was useless to remonstrate with them, he thought. Both his groom and valet had been his retainers since he was a boy. When he'd told them his plans, they had been loud in their disapproval. Richard had finally given them the choice of remaining in India, on comfortable pensions or returning to England with him. Of course both had voted to return, but not without frequent protest and admonitions and dire prophesies of doom. The trouble was, he knew both men would lay down their lives for him and had only his welfare at heart. He sighed, wishing he could make them understand how important it was for him to regain Weycross Abbey. St. Symingtons had held the Abbey since the twelfth century. Held it until seven years ago when it had been stolen from his father.

With a start, Richard realized the carriage had halted. He jumped down, telling Kirby he didn't expect to be much above half an hour, and unconsciously squared his shoulders. His call on Lady Castlereigh was in the nature of a test, and would determine, to a large extent, his acceptance by the ton.

Lady Castlereigh was entertaining when her butler discreetly handed her Richard's card. Lady Eversleigh was present with her pretty little half sister, Jenny, and Lady Brookhurst had called with her two daughters, Carolyn and Cordelia. Lady Castlereigh hesitated over introducing an unknown young man to her guests without first ascertaining his worthiness. Still, she had promised the duke.

"My dears, I hope you'll forgive me. There's a young man here, come all the way from India. The Duke of Edgecombe befriended him when he was there, and simply implored me to introduce him about."

"Do you mean Richard Danvers?" Lady Brookhurst asked eagerly. "It's all over Town that he's immensely wealthy, and come home to England to find a wife. I've been dying to meet him." She glanced at her daughters, and wished that this morning, of all mornings, Cordelia had not chosen to throw out a spot.

Lady Eversleigh spoke lightly. "I heard that both of his parents are dead. Poor boy, it must be very lonely for him. Do let us meet him." An orphan herself, she had a softness for those similarly afflicted.

Richard was shown in a few minutes later, and they were all agreeably surprised by his appearance. "Lord, he's handsome," Carolyn whispered loudly to her sister, voicing both their thoughts. If Richard heard, he gave no sign as he made an elegant bow to Lady Castlereigh. She smiled her appreciation and, with a sigh of relief, introduced him to the rest of the company. The conversation was general for a few minutes, with the usual questions of how he liked England, and wasn't he glad to be back.

"What are your plans, Mr. Danvers, if I may ask?" Lady Brookhurst enquired.

"For the present, I hope to see something of London. It's all new to me, you know. Then I must look about for a house. I hope to find something in Yorkshire, where I lived as a boy."

"It's a beautiful part of the country," Lady Eversleigh said approvingly. "We'll be going back there in a few weeks, and I hope you'll come and visit us."

"Well, I hope he won't be going North so soon," Lady Brookhurst said. "Why, the Season has just started. Now, Mr. Danvers, I'm giving a small rout party on Friday for my girls. I know it's terribly short notice, but we'd be pleased to have you come."

"Thank you, Lady Brookhurst, I'd be honoured." A disarming smile had both girls feeling near giddy with delight. Their mother, fearful that they might make cakes of themselves, announced it was time to take their leave. Lady Eversleigh rose also, and presented her hand to Richard.

"It was a pleasure to meet you, Mr. Danvers. I hope we shall see you in Yorkshire."

"Thank you, Lady Eversleigh. Your servant, Miss Eversleigh."

As the ladies were leaving, they encountered Lady Fairchild and her daughter, Elizabeth, just arriving. Lady Brookhurst was at once reluctant to go, for Elizabeth Fairchild was the toast of the current Season. She had little choice, however, and swept out the door with her girls in tow. She prayed Richard Danvers had more sense than to become infatuated with a pretty face and handsome portion. It wasn't fair the way Elizabeth had all the eligible young men lining up at her door, and the child didn't even make an effort. They simply flocked to her side like bees to honey.

Richard was standing, facing the door, when Elizabeth Fairchild entered. The sun streaming in behind her created an aura around her. Richard stared dumbly, thinking she was the most beautiful creature he had ever seen.

Conscious of his regard, Elizabeth raised her eyes to his, and he was reminded of the startled look a fawn wears when it encounters the unexpected. Her eyes were large, velvety brown, and all too soon lowered. Richard realized he'd been staring rudely.

Two older women followed her in, and Lady Castlereigh introduced them as Lady Fairchild and her aunt, Mrs. Davenport. Somehow he made the appropriate responses before making his bow to Miss Fairchild.

Mrs. Davenport reached out and poked him with her cane. He judged her to be quite ancient, but her tiny dark eyes were bright with curiosity.

"I've seen you before, young man. She—" with a nod at Lady Castlereigh "—mumbles, so I didn't catch your name."

"Richard Danvers, ma'am, but you can't have seen me before. I just arrived in England."

"Speak up, young man."

He repeated himself and she watched his lips move. "You *look* like an Englishman—where were you born, then?"

"I beg your pardon, Mrs. Davenport. I *am* English, though I left here when I was only ten."

"Thought so," she said, nodding her grey head in satisfaction. "Who were your people?"

Richard was saved from answering by Miss Fairchild. She laid a hand on her aunt's arm. "Please, Aunt Horatia, you're embarrassing the young man." To Richard she said softly, "You mustn't mind my aunt. Was she putting you through an inquisition?"

"I appear to remind her of someone," he said, laughing.

"I'll remember," Mrs. Davenport promised him. "Never forget a face. You come to tea, young man. Danvers, is it? No, that can't be right."

Elizabeth laughed, and Richard found himself unaccountably pleased by the sound. He liked the cadence of her soft voice, too.

"You'll have to change your name, Mr. Danvers, just to please my great-aunt."

The others were talking, and he took the opportunity to ask her quietly, "And what must I do to please you, Miss Fairchild?"

"Do you wish to?" she returned lightly.

"Very much so." He was as surprised as Elizabeth by the intensity of his words, and smiled to ease the tension.

"Then come and have tea with my great-aunt on Friday."

"Will you be there?"

"Of course, sir. We're staying with her while we're in Town, and she acts as my chaperon a great deal of the time."

"I see it behooves me to win over Great-Aunt Horatia. How best I go about it?"

"Change your name! I doubt else will do. She gets very stubborn when she has a notion in her head, and you probably put her in mind of someone from Harrogate."

"Harrogate?" He was startled. Perhaps Mrs. Davenport *had* recognized him, in a manner of speaking. Josiah told him he looked like his grandfather, and Harrogate was not above an hour's drive from the Abbey.

"That's where our home is," Elizabeth was saying, unaware of how much she had discomposed him. "It's a lovely part of the country, and so much more…peaceful than London. I should not own it, perhaps, but I miss it dreadfully."

"Elizabeth, darling girl, what nonsense is this?" Lady Fairchild had turned in time to hear her last comment. "Why, I vow you've not had one evening free since we arrived in Town. How could you possibly be missing home?" To Richard she explained, "We live quite retired in the country. There is hardly any socializing, and the few assemblies they get up are terribly provincial. I feel quite as though I'm in exile there."

"But, Mother—"

"Elizabeth, Aunt Horatia has nodded off. Be a good child and wake her. It's time we took our leave." Amelia Fairchild made a mental note to have a talk with her daughter. While she didn't particularly care what Mr. Danvers thought, she did not wish it spread about Town that Elizabeth would rather spend her time in the country. She dismissed Richard without a second thought. He might cut a handsome figure and possess a tidy fortune, but he wasn't titled.

Richard realized he had overstayed his first morning call and took his leave of Lady Castlereigh, thanking her warmly for receiving him. She was a kindly soul, and not averse to helping others as long as it did not require a great deal of effort on her part. By assisting Richard she would not only put the duke under obligation to her, but have all the matchmaking mamas seeking her out for an introduction to this wealthy young man. Well pleased, she invited him to dine one evening.

Richard accepted gracefully, and then made his bow to Lady Fairchild and Mrs. Davenport. Elizabeth, under her mother's watchful eye, gave him her hand. "It was a pleasure meeting you, Mr. Danvers."

"The pleasure was all mine. I shall look forward to seeing you on Friday."

"Friday? What is this?" Lady Fairchild demanded.

"*I* invited him to tea," Mrs. Davenport announced. "I trust you have no objection, Amelia?"

"No, no, Aunt, of course not. Until Friday, then, Mr. Danvers."

Lady Castlereigh stood quietly beside him, and as the door closed behind Lady Fairchild, said, "Amelia hopes to inherit her aunt's fortune, and will do nothing to displease her. If you're of a mind to pursue the lovely Elizabeth, I'd advise you to court Horatia Davenport first."

Richard grinned. He had passed his first test and won an ally in Lady Castlereigh. That would make his acceptance by the ton easier. And acceptance by the ton was the first objective in his master plan. He left the house with a buoyant step and renewed confidence.

ROSCOE WAS NOT SO EASILY persuaded. "So you managed to get yourself invited here and there. How's that going to help you find out about Lord Pembroke? Ye didn't even mention his name to those ladies."

"No, and I don't intend to. Help me off with these boots." He extended a leg, and the little valet knelt before him. "How far do you think I'd get if I started asking questions about Pembroke right off? The aristocracy protects its own. He may be a scoundrel and a thief, but they'd close ranks quick enough against any stranger who appeared asking prying questions."

Roscoe replaced the boots with soft, brocaded slippers. "Mayhap you're right, but the longer you go masquerading as plain Mr. Danvers, the more folks will resent it when they find out the truth. Lady Castlereigh won't feel kindly at being taken for a fool, and that Lady Brookhurst and Miss Fairchild you were talking about. How are they going to feel?"

Richard poured himself a small glass of wine and held the glass up to watch the sun's rays playing off the amber liquid. "If all goes well, I don't believe Lady Castlereigh will hold it against me. In fact, I think she may well be an ally. She offered me some advice before I left about courting Elizabeth Fairchild."

"Courting! Now, sir, you got no business courting a young lady—not till you get this business settled. It just ain't right."

"Cut line, Roscoe. I've no intention of courting anyone just yet... although if I had, it would certainly be Miss Fairchild. You never saw such a beauty. Skin so fair and delicate that one can almost see the blue blood running beneath it. And eyes... liquid brown pools I swear a man could drown in. I looked into those eyes and for a moment I forgot everything else, and stared at her like any Johnny raw."

Roscoe groaned aloud at his master's dreamy expression. "Not again! That's just the way you took on about that Miss Victorie, and look at the mess that landed you in."

Richard laughed and swung an arm round his valet. "That was a very different thing. Victoria knew every trick ever devised to enslave a man, and she used them all. Miss Fairchild is a sweet girl, and I'll swear not an ounce of deceit in her."

"Aye, and I recollect that's just about what ye said when you first met Miss Victorie. A poor misunderstood thing, she was—according to you."

Richard laughed. "Do you give me no credit for becoming wiser with my years? I was a green lad then, and Victoria the first woman to ever flatter me with her attention. It would have been wonderful if she had not turned my head. I'm not likely to be so gullible again."

"Ha! Why, if old Danvers hadn't put Lord Weymouth in her path, like as not you'd be leg-shackled to her, and ruing the day you cast eyes on her. I'd not wager a halfpenny on you if she was to turn up in London and start throwing out lures to you—which is just the sort of thing she would do once she learnt you inherited Danvers's pile and have a title to boot."

"What a cynic you've become, but rest your mind. Victoria *has* a husband, as you so discreetly reminded me."

"Aye, and that she-witch would find a way to get shed of him quick enough, if an it suited her. Like a black-widow spider, that one."

"We disagree enough as it is. Let's not come to daggers over Victoria. It's unlikely we shall ever see her again. As for Elizabeth Fairchild, you need have no fears. She is as different from Victoria as…as day from night."

"As you say, sir. 'Tis no business of mine if you choose to mislead a sweet young lady with this deception."

"Ah, I thought we would come back to that sooner or later. What a trial I must be to you. At least I can relieve you of my troublesome presence for one evening. Lay out suitable clothes, please. I believe I shall dine out tonight."

"Dine out?" Roscoe was incredulous. "And where might ye be going, not knowing a soul in this town, and not belonging to any of the gentlemen's clubs? As sure as—"

"Roscoe, I understand that you and Kirby consider yourselves my guardians, but I am a grown man. I have attained my majority, and I really am quite capable of looking after myself—no matter what the pair of you believe. Now, please lay out raiment, and not another word, or like as not, I won't come home at all."

Under that dire threat, his man busied himself about the room. He swept forth an ivory coat from the armoire and flung it across the bed. Richard watched, amused, as the matching waistcoat followed it. Boots were handled more tenderly, for the valet took loving pride in their glossiness, but the stack of linen neckcloths were tossed haphazardly upon the bed.

"Enough! I think I shall do better without your assistance. Take yourself off, and under no circumstances are you to wait up for me."

Richard was hard put not to smile as Roscoe bowed himself from the room, without a word. His servitude wouldn't last, he knew. His valet would be in the room first thing in the morning, demanding an account of his evening. Well, his plans were no more extensive than dropping in at one of the new coffee houses, and perhaps the pit section of Covent Garden. The duke had advised him that all the young bucks could be found of an evening at the Garden. He might pick up some useful rumours there.

Richard found Kirby waiting for him as he prepared to leave the house, and was forced to listen to a quarter-hour harangue on the dangers of being alone and afoot in London. Nevertheless, it was a warm, balmy evening, and he insisted on strolling. Kirby joined Roscoe in his wrath over their young master, bemoaning his mulishness. But between curses over his stubbornness, they both prayed for his safe return. Neither intended to retire before Richard was seen to be safely home.

The young lord put them both from his mind, knowing there was little he could do to ease their concern. He walked along leisurely, wondering at the new gas lights which gave the avenue an eerie glow, and did little to illuminate the street. Carriages crowded the road, and he

realized he was wise in walking, for he made much better time than most of the carriages.

Turning off the square, he walked north, hoping he
was heading in the direction of the coffee house he'd
noted on their arrival. The streets looked vastly different
in the dusky light, and the farther he walked, the more
certain he became that he had erred in his direction.
There were few carriages to be seen now, and the town-
houses were not brightly lit as they had been on the
square. As he approached a crossroads, Richard decided
to turn east again, and try to circle back to the more
fashionable area. This avenue appeared even more de-
serted than the north road, and he looked uneasily
around him. He blamed Kirby for his unrest, putting
notions of cutthroats and footpads in his head.

Whistling to lift his spirits, Richard quickened his step
and tightened his grip on his walking stick. A few blocks
away lay stylish, elegant London. Here, even in the dark,
he sensed the poverty and desperation. Every sense alert
to danger, he imagined eyes watching him from the
darkness. A loud curse broke the stillness, and Richard
strained to see. Just ahead, in the mouth of an alleyway,
a scuffle was afoot. He cautiously drew closer, and it appeared one man had been set upon by three stalwarts.
Richard saw him land a nice left to the jaw of one of the
thugs, but another had circled behind and hefted a heavy
club.

"Watch your back!" he yelled. The man heard him
and turned in time to ward off the blow with his raised
arm. Richard saw him stagger and fall, and feared his
arm was broken.

He reached the footpad a second later. Grabbing him
roughly by the shoulder, Richard spun him round. A
punishing right to the stomach doubled the man over in

agony. Richard, wielding his own cane, turned to face the others. Apparently feeling two against three were not good enough odds, they were running from the alley.

"Cowards," he called after them. And then, unexpectedly, a sharp pain pierced his shoulder. "What the...?" He turned again, slowly. The man he'd left lying on the ground stood a few feet away.

"That'll teach you to meddle, me fine lord," he muttered before chasing after his friends.

Slightly dazed, Richard took a few seconds to realize he'd been knifed. The blade was still in his right shoulder. Sinking to his knees, he tried to reach the handle with his left hand. Although he could feel it, he couldn't grip it well enough to remove it. He eyed the man he'd tried to help. To all appearances, he lay sleeping peacefully. Richard crawled towards him, pain throbbing through his shoulder with every movement. He ignored the pain, thinking that if they didn't get shut of this place soon, thieves would be on them like a pack of wild dogs.

The man had not stirred. He was younger than Richard had at first supposed, and he guessed they were of an age. Judging by his clothes, he was either a member of the peerage or very wealthy. Richard shook the man's shoulder roughly.

The young gentleman opened his eyes slowly. For an instant, he stared uncomprehendingly at the face above him. Then a wide grin split his face.

"I believe we shall be friends. If I keep visiting gaming hells, I shall need a friend with a right faster than lightning. Edward Salford at your service, sir." He attempted to sit up, groaning as he put weight on his left arm.

"Let's skip the introductions for now," Richard said. "It's more important we get quit of this place. No doubt your arm's broken, and I've a knife in my shoulder. Do you think we can—"

"A knife! Here, let me see—"

"Leave it," Richard gasped. "We need to reach safety first. I think, perhaps, if we support each other..."

With Richard's left arm round Salford's right shoulder, they managed to stagger to their feet. Salford looked around him, trying to recall where he was. Nodding, he told Richard, "Only a stone's throw to Fordham Road. From there we should be able to get a hackney."

Leaning against each other, they made their way to the foot of the alley. Richard scanned the street. No one was in sight. Still, he knew instinctively that hidden eyes were watching from the darkened windows of the tenements. And if they should realize they were wounded...

"Do you know a good fighting song?" he whispered to Salford.

His companion, intoxicated enough not to wonder at the strange question, responded instantly. "The Glory of the Ninth. It's my cousin's regiment. Why? Do you have a duet in mind? Are we going to serenade the watch?"

"Start us off, and I'll follow your lead. If we're lucky, anyone watching will think we've only had a bit much to drink. Sing as loud as you can."

Salford lifted his voice, and after a moment Richard echoed his words. Their steps in no way resembled a military cadence, but the song proclaimed their willingness to do battle. Perhaps it was that alone which held the watchers at bay.

Richard stumbled and prayed he wouldn't pass out before they found a carriage. Salford's voice faltered. The reality of warm blood saturating his fingers where they gripped his friend's shoulder sobered him abruptly. They were near the corner of Fordham now, and he heard the sound of a carriage rumbling over the rough stones. His piercing whistle brought the hackney to a halt, and Salford urged Richard towards it. Behind them, he heard running footsteps.

CHAPTER TWO

SALFORD AND RICHARD were within six feet of the carriage when the driver brought his team to a halt. He eyed the two young men who were looking drunk or worse, and the half dozen footpads giving chase. He hesitated before lifting his arm a fraction. Salford yelled, "Move one inch and I'll hunt you down like a bloody fox!" The driver stayed his hand, nervously urging them to hurry.

Salford had the door open, and half-lifted, half-shoved Richard in. His own boot barely cleared the ground when the driver jerked the reins, and the old carriage jolted forward. The young man fell in and just managed to pull the door shut with his good arm. Vile curses filled the air as the ruffians found themselves balked of their prey.

Richard, mercifully, was unconscious, and Salford left him lying where he had fallen across the seat. He thought it kinder not to revive him. Using his handkerchief, he applied pressure around the knife handle. In only minutes the piece of linen was soaked. Worrying over the amount of blood the man was losing, Salford rapped on the carriage ceiling with Richard's cane.

As soon as the coach halted, he jumped out to confer with the driver. He was in a quandary. Obviously his benefactor needed the attentions of a doctor, and he didn't know where to find one. The driver was of no help. Nothing for it, Salford thought, but to take the man home with him. He gave the driver his direction, and then shuddered. The duchess was not going to like this.

When the hackney at last came to a rumbling halt in front of No. 2 Belgrave Square, Salford blessed his good fortune. The house was quiet and only dimly lit, which meant his mother was out for the evening. Now all he needed was Simmonds. Simmonds would know what to do. He grinned, wondering if this mess would overset their stoic butler. As boys, he and his brother had never tired of trying to rattle the phlegmatic Simmonds. They had baited him endlessly—without result. Well, if Simmonds took this in stride, he'd give it up.

"You, there," he called up to the driver, "Get down and give me a hand."

"Jest be paying me, guv, and I'll be on my way and none the wiser."

"You yellow-livered jaw dog. Get down here at once and give me a hand. The man inside is wounded—unless you'd rather I leave him in your carriage?"

That brought the driver scrambling down. With much head-shaking and dire predictions, he reluctantly helped Salford get Richard up the steps of the impressive townhouse. Before Salford could search for his key, the door was opened.

"Good evening, Lord Edward," the butler greeted him calmly, although his small, round eyes were focused on the driver and the unconscious man between them.

"Simmonds! Just the man I wanted. My friend here is—"

"Perhaps you'd care to go into the details later, sir?" the butler interrupted smoothly, with a nod at the driver.

"Oh, right you are. Pay him off for me, will you, Simmonds? And don't argue. We've been through rather a lot."

If the butler heard him, he gave no sign of it. He dealt with the driver rapidly, his considerable dignity intimidating the smaller man. Edward watched appreciatively. His mother always said that Simmonds, with his hawk nose and silver hair, looked more like a duke than his father ever had.

Simmonds, easily supporting Richard against his broad frame, turned to him. "May I suggest we put your friend in the Blue Room?"

"Excellent. Here, let me help you. Handle him gently, Simmonds—he's been wounded."

"Really, sir? And I thought the knife protruding from his coat was merely a new fancy of the Town Set."

Salford didn't answer. The pain in his own arm had him grinding his teeth. But that would have to wait for even in the dim light of the hall the man looked deathly pale. They managed, with Richard between them, to get him into the chamber at the rear of the first floor—the room most removed from the duchess's apartments. Simmonds manoeuvred him onto the bed, face down. Directing Edward to provide more light, he bent to examine the wound. There wasn't any way to determine the extent of the damage until Richard's coat and shirt were cut away, and he wouldn't chance trying to remove the knife until he could see the wound more clearly.

"Find Findley and sent him in at once. Also, Mrs. Chambers."

"Not Nanna—"

"Mrs. Chambers," he repeated, "and tell her I shall need a pair of shears."

"But Simmonds—"

"If you value your friend's life, Lord Edward, I should not waste time arguing."

Salford closed his mouth and hurried from the room. Findley was no problem. His father's groom could always be found in his quarters above the stables. Salford could even understand why Simmonds wanted him. Findley had served as his father's batman during his prestigious army career. He knew Findley had a great knowledge of wounds. But why on earth did he want Nanna?

His old nurse, now acting as a sort of companion to the duchess, would be in her room. She treated him and his brother as though they were still tykes in leading strings, and she would certainly scold him for this night's work. Salford was tempted to go to his own room and change his dress before approaching her, but mindful of Simmonds's warning, he hurried along the hall. He might have been fearless on the dueling field, but he had to screw up his courage to tap on her door.

It was opened almost instantly. "Master Edward! I know you're not paying your old nurse a social call. What mischief have you afoot?"

"Nanna, I haven't time to explain. Simmonds needs you in the Blue Room at once. Oh, and he said to bring a pair of shears."

She studied him a moment, wondering if he was playing off one of his tricks. The grey eyes in the old and wrinkled face were still lively and full of intelligence. After a moment, she gave a satisfied nod. "I'll be there directly; however, I suggest you change your attire before the duchess returns and sees you looking such a fright." The door closed firmly, her words lingering in the air.

So Nanna expected his mother back soon. The fat would be in the fire then. He hurried to his own chambers and found his man waiting for him. The servants' grapevine was a thing of marvel.

"Evening, Dawes. Get me a brandy and then help me get out of these clothes."

"My lord! What have you done to your coat, sir? I doubt that it will ever come clean."

"Doesn't matter. I think I broke my arm, and you'll have to cut the coat off me. And hurry, I have to get back downstairs."

When Salford returned to the Blue Room, he wore knee breeches with a soft, white linen shirt. The full sleeves came down to his knuckles, and he hoped it would help disguise the arm dangling limply at his side. The brandy had helped to make the pain at least bearable.

Simmonds glanced at him briefly and then bent over the young man on the bed. "Findley removed the knife and dressed the wound. I think your friend will do; however, we've sent for Dr. Halymont. Mrs. Chambers has gone to the kitchen to make your friend a posset, and will remain here to nurse him—at least until the duchess returns."

Salford stepped closer. To his untrained eyes, the man on the bed still looked near death, although the removal of the knife was a decided improvement.

"Is there someone we should notify, my lord?"

Salford looked at the butler blankly.

"Your friend's family, perhaps?"

"Oh. Well, the truth is, I don't know who he is."

Simmonds said nothing, his brows arching slightly.

"I know it must seem odd—I bring home a strange man with a knife in his back—but I am obligated to him. He probably saved my life."

The duchess appeared in the doorway in time to hear her son's words. "Edward!"

Her cry swung both men round instantly. "Your Grace—" Simmonds bowed, while Salford hurried forward.

"Mama, don't be alarmed. I'm perfectly safe." Without thinking, he stretched out both hands to her. She caught the agony in his eyes as he moved his arm, and then had to let if fall again, his face deathly pale.

"Simmonds, a chair for my son, please. What have you done to your arm?" Her face, almost a mirror image of his own, regarded him with loving concern.

"It's nothing serious, Mama, I promise you."

She nodded and began to roll up his sleeve. In spite of herself, a small gasp escaped her lips at the sight of his bruised and swollen arm. "How did this happen?"

The duchess continued to stand, and though she only reached five foot in height, she seemed to tower above him. He skipped over the fact that he'd been in a notorious gaming hell and was more than a little intoxicated. "Three footpads jumped me, and I was holding them off pretty well when one of them managed to get behind me. He was going to hit me over the head with a club when the man over there yelled a warning. I spun round and got my arm up to block the blow." He grimaced. "I'm afraid it's broken. I would've been done for if he hadn't interfered. He's got a right—I beg your pardon, Mama. Well, he held them off. I was fairly useless with only one arm." Salford swallowed. No point in mentioning that he'd been unconscious and in his cups as well. "I didn't see precisely how it happened, but he took a knife in the shoulder for his pains. I couldn't leave him there, could I? So I brought him home. I knew Simmonds would know what to do."

The duchess said nothing. She walked across the room and stood staring at the man resting on the bed. Looking at his face in profile, she felt a vague start of recognition. She looked closer. No, she didn't know the young man, although there was something familiar about him. "Who is he, Edward?"

"That's just it, Mama. I don't know, else I would've taken him to his own home."

Simmonds, who had discreetly effaced himself into the background, coughed and stepped forward. "Excuse me, Your Grace. I took the liberty of checking the gentleman's pockets. He was carrying calling cards." He extended a card to her.

The duchess glanced at it. "Richard Danvers. I'm positive I don't know him, and yet it seems I've heard the name recently."

"It's very possible, Your Grace. I believe this is the young gentleman recently arrived from India. Rumour has it that he is immensely wealthy and has come home to England to seek a wife."

The duchess nodded. "And does your knowledge extend so far as an address?"

"Yes, Your Grace. I understand he is leasing Lord Batterton's townhouse."

"I see. Edward, I should like you to escort me to my rooms. Simmonds, please remain with Mr. Danvers until Mrs. Chambers returns. You have sent for Dr. Halymont?" Simmonds nodded, and she continued, "Thank you. Please advise me when the doctor arrives."

Salford knew he was in for it. His mother would never rake him down in front of the servants, but what she might choose to say in the privacy of her rooms was another matter.

The duchess dismissed her dresser as soon as they entered her apartment. She waited quietly until the door closed behind the woman, and then motioned for her son to be seated.

"There are several aspects regarding your conduct this evening which give me grave concern. May I enquire where you were when this attack took place?"

He was not fool enough to think she was literally asking his permission, and answered her quietly, "Near Fordham Road, ma'am. I was on my way to meet Fitzhugh and—"

"Fordham Road? As I recollect, that is rather a shabby area. What, precisely, were you doing on foot in such a neighbourhood?"

"The truth is I heard about this new gaming house, and thought I'd give it a look. Fitzhugh said—"

"A gaming *hell!* Really, Edward." She paused, searching for words. "I find it difficult to conceive that a son of mine has so little resolution, so little character, that he is content to squander his inheritance. Not to mention a shameful waste of your time and intelligence. Can you find nothing better to do with your leisure hours?"

"I am truly sorry to have upset you so much, Mama, but all the gentlemen in Town—"

She turned on him in a fury. "I have no wish to hear what other gentlemen may or may not do. You are a Salford. Much more is expected of you. Almost, you convince me that your father is right. He has long held that you stand in need of more responsibility. Perhaps if you were to manage one of the estate farms in the North—"

"Mama—you cannot mean it."

"I am quite serious, Edward. This evening has convinced me that something must be done. Do you even begin to comprehend that if not for a stranger's intervention, you might have been killed?'' Her voice broke on the last word, and he moved at once to her side.

The duchess waved him away. "No, I do not want your charming apologies or empty promises. You have endangered your own life through your carelessness, and though that may mean little enough to you, you are also responsible for that young man belowstairs. Imagine for a moment, if you will, how you would have felt if he had died.''

Her words chilled him. She had no way of knowing that fear for Danvers's life had been driving him, and he walked to the window casement.

"Do not misunderstand me, Edward. However thankful I am that he is alive, we are now under an obligation to him. A wealthy provincial who is, no doubt, seeking an entrée into Polite Society.''

A tap on the door interrupted them, and at a nod from the duchess, Edward thankfully opened it. It was Simmonds.

"Please excuse me, Your Grace. I thought you'd like to know that Dr. Halymont is belowstairs, and the young man is conscious.''

"Thank you, Simmonds. I shall be down directly. Edward, go with Simmonds and have the doctor look at your arm.''

He hesitated for a second before striding across the room to her side. Bending, he gently kissed her cheek. "I beg your forgiveness, Mama. I would never, willingly, do anything to cause you pain.''

Her eyes softened instantly, though her voice was brisk. "Be off with you. We will discuss this when we are both calmer.''

It was a half-hour before the duchess returned to the Blue Room. She carried herself, as always, regally, and entered with a ready smile that belied the inner turmoil she was feeling. Pausing in the doorway, she surveyed the room.

Richard Danvers was sitting on the bed, helpless, while Mrs. Chambers and Dr. Halymont endeavoured to wrap him in a voluminous nightshirt. His eyes met hers across the room, and he grinned at the ludicrous picture he must have presented. The duchess almost returned the smile. There was something about the man which reminded her of someone. An elusive, fleeting memory which she couldn't identify.

Edward, seeing her in the doorway, called to her. "Will you come and meet my rescuer? Mother, may I present Mr. Richard Danvers. Mr. Danvers, my mother, the Duchess of Cardiff."

If Richard was discomfitted by the exalted company he had fallen into, it did not show. "Your Grace," he said with a nod. "Please forgive me for not rising. I had hoped to meet you under more favourable circumstances. The Duke of Edgecombe spoke of you often."

"There could hardly be more favourable conditions, Mr. Danvers. I am extremely grateful to you for saving my son's life."

"I fear that's a bit of an exaggeration. He was set on by some petty thieves. If I hadn't interfered, they would have bashed him over the head and stolen his purse. As it is, I am the one who stands in his debt."

She gave him a full smile now, pleased with what she saw and heard. "We will not quarrel over it." Turning to the doctor, she enquired about his shoulder.

"Fortunately, he seems to have a strong constitution. Findley did a proper job patching him up, and time will do the rest. A few days in bed, and then if he takes it easy for a month or two, he should do fine."

"And Edward?"

"Broken arm. I've set it, and if you can convince him to keep it in the sling, it should mend well enough. I'll want another look at it in a fortnight."

While the duchess spoke with the doctor, and their attention was focused on Edward, Richard slid gingerly from the bed. His legs felt like rubber, and he braced himself against the side of the bed, taking a deep breath. He wondered if the duchess's gratitude would extend to lending him a carriage. He needed to get home before Roscoe had an army of servants out combing the streets for him.

"Mr. Danvers!" the duchess cried. "What are you doing standing? Did not you hear the doctor? You need several days in bed."

"It's what I had in mind, Your Grace. If you could have a carriage convey me—"

"What nonsense is this? Has the blow to your shoulder addled your brain? You are in no condition to be moved. You will remain here until that wound has healed sufficiently. I will not hear of anything else."

"I appreciate your kindness, but I cannot put you to so much trouble. Besides, my servants will be worried if I don't return home. They...they have been with me since I was a boy, and sometimes act as though—"

"Say no more, I understand perfectly," Edward interrupted with a knowing look at Nanna.

"It's unnecessary in any case," the duchess added. "I sent a note to your townhouse so your people will not be concerned by your absence."

There was a sudden commotion in the hall, and Richard, weak and dizzy as he was, grinned at the sound of one strident voice raised above the others. He had tried to warn the duchess.

"I don't care if the King of England lives here, you old windbag. And if you don't get out of my way, I'll knock you on your—"

Richard quickly raised his voice. "I believe that's my man. I apologize, Your Grace, but he won't rest until he's seen me."

The duchess moved towards the door. Simmonds was blocking the hall and a small leprechaun of a man was trying to dodge around him. In a brilliant move, the little man dived between Simmonds's legs and slid several feet down the hall. The duchess stared down at him.

Coming to a stop, Roscoe looked up at the elegant lady standing before him. He knew instantly that this must be the duchess who had sent the note. He hastily removed his cap, a comical look of dismay crossing his features. "Beg your pardon, Your Grace," he mumbled, scrambling to his feet and awkwardly bowing at the same time.

"I tried to stop him, Your Grace," Simmonds said, coming up behind him.

"Thank you, Simmonds. That will be all." The butler allowed himself one contemptuous look at Roscoe before bowing and withdrawing. She motioned to the intruder. "I take it you are here to see Mr. Danvers. This way, if you please."

The duchess swept back into the room, and Roscoe followed. Several people there stared at him, but his eyes went directly to Richard, still leaning against the bed, and Richard was not looking pleased to see him.

"Mr. Danvers, sir, I...that is, me and Kirby thought..."

"What? Is Kirby here, too?"

"Yes, sir. He's out in the carriage, sir. He was...uh, worried, sir, and—"

Richard turned to the duchess, who was trying hard not to smile. "If you will excuse me, Your Grace, my man can help me to dress, and he'll see me home."

"I won't hear of it. You are in no condition to be moved, Mr. Danvers, as I'm sure Dr. Halymont will agree. Your man may stay and help put you to bed. Simmonds will find accommodations for him, and for your groom as well."

"I think you should listen to the duchess, young man," the doctor added. "You lost a great deal of blood. I won't be responsible for your condition if you insist on moving."

He was almost too tired to argue further, but he knew the disruption Roscoe and Kirby would cause in any well-run house. And neither would agree to leaving him there. Richard stood up and took a step forward. "Really, Your Grace, I feel much—" the words trailed off as he pitched forward in a dead faint. The room evolved into chaos. His head rested on the hem of the duchess's dress. Roscoe dived forward at once to kneel beside him, and glared at Mrs. Chambers, who knelt on the other side.

"I knew this would happen," the doctor said. "These young men won't listen to their elders. They seem to think they're invincible. I won't be responsible if he won't follow my orders."

Edward interrupted him. "Yes, doctor, we know, but Danvers won't be going anywhere tonight. Help his man get him back in bed."

Mrs. Chambers stepped back to allow them room. "It was my posset. It makes one feel much stronger than one really is. It's my fault if he overestimated his strength. I shall stay here and nurse him."

"I'll be the one nursing him, ma'am," Roscoe was quick to inform her. "I've been doing so since he was ten. He don't need no one else."

"Nonsense. Everyone knows a man needs a woman's touch when he is ill. Men are too clumsy." She appealed to the duchess, "Your Grace, tell this man—" She broke off in mid-sentence, her mouth hanging open as she stared at the door, and the others turned to see what had silenced her. The room grew still, and as though frozen in place, no one moved. The Duke of Cardiff stood framed in the doorway.

CHAPTER THREE

THE DUKE OF CARDIFF was frequently described as a distinguished-looking gentleman. His hair had greyed at the temples, and as he eschewed wigs, it was brushed back in waves which most ladies deemed attractive. He had a wide forehead with heavy brows over dark hooded eyes—eyes quite capable of intimidating lesser men.

Everything about him, from his short but powerful frame, to the well-cut, expensive clothes he wore, underscored his air of forcefulness. The duke, accustomed to leading men and dictating their movements, was not a person to be approached easily. He preferred order above all, and his servants were said to be the most discreet and efficient in London.

It was, perhaps, understandable, then, that he was astonished by the disorder before him. The duchess came at once to his side and placed a hand lightly on his arm.

"Justin, this is a surprise. We had not looked to see you before tomorrow."

"Not an unpleasant one, I trust?" He murmured, continuing to gaze at Roscoe and Dr. Halymont, as they manoeuvred Richard back onto the bed.

"Of course not, dear. Have you eaten? Come into the Long Drawingroom and I'll order a tray for you while I tell you what has been happening." She persuaded Justin to leave with her and, with a backward glance at their son, added, "Pray, take care of our guest."

Relieved of his father's presence, Edward collapsed into a chair. "What rotten luck. Father would choose today to come home."

Roscoe threw him a contemptuous glance. It mattered little to him what the duke did or thought. His first concern was, and always would be, for Richard. He ignored Edward and addressed the woman hovering over his charge. "If you will be excusing us, ma'am, I'll be making my master more comfortable."

Mrs. Chambers sniffed. "Mr. Danvers is now a guest in this house, and I'll be hearing what the doctor has to say before leaving him in the care of a wee fellow like you."

Dr. Halymont was packing his gear. He'd had quite enough of Cardiff House for one evening. "Just try to keep the man quiet. He needs rest now more than anything else. I suspect he'll not regain consciousness before morning. Give him some gruel or broth then, and nothing heavier for the next few days. And you, young man," he said, glaring at Edward, "keep that arm in the sling, and don't be trying nothing strenuous. Now, if you'll excuse me—"

Lord Edward rose wearily and walked out with the doctor.

Mrs. Chambers, whispering, motioned to Roscoe. "I'll look in on him in the morning, and if he's awake, I'll make some of my special restorative broth. Now if you'll come with me, Mr.—I beg your pardon, but I don't believe I caught your name. I am Mrs. Chambers."

"Roscoe Bertinelli, but I ain't going nowhere. I'll be staying right here with Mr. Danvers."

"An Italian. I might've known. My sister married an Italian, and a life of misery he led her. A more contrary, quarrelsome man I never met. However, that's neither here nor there. I was only going to suggest that I show you the way to your room. Then you may come back here and check on your master."

"I'll be sleeping right here. You can have a cot moved in here, or if not, I'll just sleep in that chair."

"Hmmph. Just like my brother-in-law." But she accorded him a grudging respect for his determination to remain. "If he should wake and you need assistance, ring for a footman and have them rouse me at once."

Roscoe spent an uncomfortable night on the cot two footmen had carried in, at Mrs. Chambers's orders. It was to no avail. Richard didn't regain consciousness. The little valet spent two more harrowing days at Cardiff House while his master lay on the bed, barely stirring. Dr. Halymont spoke of bleeding him, and the duchess and Mrs. Chambers discussed the merits of several remedies. Edward was seen to lose several pounds in his worry over his friend and stayed close to the house. But it was Roscoe who suffered the most. He blamed his incautious tongue for driving Richard out of the house alone, and maintained a vigil by Richard's side, excepting a few minutes here and there when nature called.

It was during one of those rare instances that Richard finally regained consciousness. Mrs. Chambers had just relieved Roscoe, and was feeling the patient's brow for signs of a fever, when Richard opened his eyes. He was groggy, only vaguely remembered the fight and had no notion where he was, or who the strange woman standing over him might be.

"Ah, there. It's right glad I am to see you rejoining us, Mr. Danvers. You gave us quite a fright. Just lie still now, and I'll be fetching your man, who's just stepped out for a moment."

Richard lay still, trying to recall what had happened. His thoughts were in a muddle and he only knew that he felt weak as a kitten. Then Roscoe was there before him.

"It's about time you quit sleeping your head off. I've better things to do than hang about here waiting for you to wake up." The suspicious moisture in the valet's eyes gave the lie to the roughness of his words.

"What happened, Roscoe? I barely remember a fight, and a duchess. Was I dreaming?"

"Nay, the young lord you rescued brought you home with him, and they patched you up right enough. Then you pitched forward and went clean out of your head. I've been watching over you ever since."

"Ever since when? How long have I been here?"

"Well, this is Friday, and you went out Wednesday evening."

"Good Lord! I've been unconscious two days?" Richard tried to ease himself up.

"Take it easy, sir. Let me prop you up. Mrs. Chambers went off to get you some broth, if you feel like a bit of something."

"I'm famished. Who's Mrs. Chambers?"

Roscoe explained and by that time Nanna was back with the promised broth. She and Roscoe watched over Richard like a pair of broody hens with their chick as he ate. Word of Richard's revival passed quickly through the house, and the duchess and Edward soon appeared. Richard, a trifle embarrassed by his unkempt condition, was soon put at ease by the graciousness of the duchess and the outright gratitude of Edward.

They spent a pleasant half hour until the duchess, observing Richard was growing tired, made to leave. "If there is anything you need, or any service we can perform for you, please let us know. It is quite settled you are to remain our guest until you've fully recovered. Don't argue, Mr. Danvers. You'll recall what happened the last time you tried that." She gave him one of her warm smiles, and Richard, absurdly weak and tired, could not disagree.

The duchess strolled down the hall with Edward, remarking, "I'm excessively glad your friend is recovering. Your father has invited a number of guests to stay next week, and it would be awkward with an invalid in the house."

"You're not anxious to get rid of him, are you, Mother? I don't think he'd be an embarrassment. His manners seem unexceptionable."

"His manners are delightful. No, I've no fault with Mr. Danvers, but it would still be awkward. The men coming are mostly political allies of your father's, and would be ill at ease with a stranger among them."

They continued to discuss their guests for a few minutes before the duchess posed a question that had been bothering her. "Now that Mr. Danvers has regained consciousness, will you be going out this evening?"

Edward smiled, "What? Tired of my company so soon?"

"Don't be ridiculous, Edward. It's merely that I must inform Cook. I am always pleased when you choose to dine with us, but you have rarely done so this past year, and now that your friend is recovering..."

"You may tell Cook to lay a cover for me, Mama. I do have a few matters to attend to this afternoon, but I'm certain I shall be back in good time." Something in her manner as she looked at him prompted him to add, "I've been a sad trial to you, haven't I?"

She laughed up at him. She could not help it. She was so pleased to see him looking his old self, with bright, clear eyes, and behaving so thoughtfully. "No, darling boy. You have been, on occasion, obstinate, frequently careless and sometimes thoughtless, but never a trial to me."

The duchess left him, light-hearted and immensely pleased with this new Edward. Perhaps his friend's close brush with death had shaken Edward enough to refrain from his habitual drinking and gambling.

Edward had cancelled several engagements he'd made prior to Danvers's accident. It occurred to him now that Richard might have also made engagements . . . engagements he could no longer keep. He hurried back to the Blue Room and stuck his head round the door. Richard was resting, but not asleep and motioned for him to enter.

"I don't mean to disturb you, but I have to go out for a bit. Is there anyone you'd like me to notify of your accident? Any appointments that you need cancelled?"

"I don't think so. I've only been in London a matter of days, and—oh, Lord. I clean forgot about Miss Fairchild!"

"Elizabeth Fairchild? Don't tell me you know Lizzie."

"Barely. I met her Wednesday at Lady Castlereigh's. Her aunt, an older woman . . . Davenport? . . . asked me to tea this afternoon."

"Don't give it another thought, old man. I'll pop in there while I'm out and explain matters. Lizzie will understand. She's a great girl."

The warmth of his voice and the familiarity with which he spoke of Miss Fairchild gave Richard pause. "Is she a particular friend of yours?"

"You might say so. She's my second cousin. Lizzie and I spent many a summer together. She might be the toast of the Town now, but I still see her as the pigtailed brat who trailed after me and my brother.''

Richard experienced a pang of jealousy, which he told himself was absurd. He barely knew the girl. In a harsher voice than he intended, he asked Edward to express his regrets.

His new friend grinned. "It didn't take you long to find the prettiest girl in Town. Now, is there anything else?''

Roscoe coughed. "Excuse me, sir, but happened you mentioned a rout party for this evening.''

"Oh, Lord, yes. Lady Bookhurst? Brockhurst? I met her at Lady Castlereigh's, too. She said she was giving a rout party for her two girls.''

"Ah, that would be Lady Brookhurst. Pair of homely-looking girls she's got to get off her hands. She'll be disappointed to lose two fine-looking specimens like us. I sent my regrets yesterday.''

"I hope you're not cancelling any engagements on my behalf, Lord Edward. I assure you, it's not at all necessary.''

"Maybe not for you, but it's dashed convenient for me. And call me Edward. By the by, do you play chess? I thought you might give me a game this evening.''

"I'm agreeable, as long as you don't expect too much. The way my mind keeps fogging over, I probably won't give you much of a game.''

"All the better—I rather like winning. I'll see you after dinner, then.'' With a wave of his good hand, he was gone, and Richard stared after him thoughtfully.

He had, unfortunately, ample time to think. He was left to his own devices for most of the afternoon, although he allowed Roscoe to shave him, and then endured an endless hour of bickering between his valet and

Mrs. Chambers. In desperation, he finally sent Roscoe off to procure clean clothes for him, and requested Mrs. Chambers to make some of her special restorative.

Settling back against the pillows, he closed his eyes, relishing the pure peace and quiet of the moment. All too soon, Mrs. Chambers returned.

"Here you are, young man. This will soon have you back on your feet quick enough."

"Thank you, Mrs. Chambers. If you'll just leave it there, I'm sure I can manage."

"If you say so, sir, but I'd be more than happy to feed it to you. No sense putting a strain on that shoulder."

"You're too kind," Richard murmured, eyeing the foul-smelling broth, "but I wouldn't dream of imposing on you. I'm certain you must have more important matters to attend to."

"Now don't you be worrying over me," she said with a laugh. "My boys are all grown now, and the truth is, I've precious little to do." She settled her sparse frame into the rocker, preparing for a comfortable cose.

Richard saw nothing for it. Praying the broth wouldn't taste as vile as it smelled, he gingerly took a spoonful. It was all he could do not to grimace at the bitter-tasting brew. Mrs. Chambers was watching him closely. He struggled for something polite to say. "It reminds me of a concoction my great-aunt used to make."

"Any lady worth her salt knows how to make a good restorative. Mind you, I don't claim it tastes good, but it'll put you back in spirits. Why, when the boys were wee lads, and ailing, just one dose of my broth would turn the trick. You wouldn't credit how quick they recovered. Eat it up, now, while it's still hot."

She was so anxious to be of help that Richard could not bring himself to offend her. Reluctantly, he reached for the spoon just as the duchess, with Dr. Halymont in tow, appeared in the door. One glance into the room was sufficient to alert her to Richard's predicament.

"Mrs. Chambers, I think we'd best leave Dr. Halymont alone with his patient. He wishes to examine Mr. Danvers's shoulder."

Richard's relief was such that he gladly submitted to the doctor's probing examination of his wound. He asked only that Halymont dump the repulsive broth out the window.

Dr. Halymont, much more himself than on their previous meeting, chuckled as he complied. "Have you noticed the exquisite roses outside this window? I do believe they thrive on Mrs. Chambers's restorative broth. Many a bowl of this stuff has been fed to the roses."

"I'm surprised it hasn't killed them—vile-tasting stuff. How soon can I return home, Doctor?"

"I would think that if you continue to improve, a few more days should see you fit. The wound's healing nicely, but you still need to rest. However, I shall inform Mrs. Chambers that you may have a more substantial diet."

"For that you have my gratitude, but I don't understand why it's taking me so long to get my strength back. Usually nothing keeps me down."

"Hmm. Well, the body's a mysterious thing. Sometimes even we doctors don't know why one heals and gets well, while another sickens and dies. I have noticed one thing, however. Those with heavy hearts don't recover near as fast as others. Nothing preying on your mind, is there?"

Richard grinned. "You weren't acquainted with my stepfather, Josiah, were you? He used to say that a thirst for revenge would eat away a man's soul and rot his body."

"Sounds like a wise man. I heard a parson speak once, and though I'm not given to regular church-going, his words made an impression on me. He said that if one would be happy and content in this life, one must first cleanse the soul of all envy, hatred and resentment. Only then could the body function as it was intended. As a doctor, I find it an interesting theory. It is possible, perhaps, that a crushing hatred could pull so much energy from the mind and body, that the body itself would be at risk." He paused, and chuckled again. "But I don't think we need worry in your case. You're much too young to have developed that sort of hatred."

He left his patient to muse on his words. Richard, after a few moments, dismissed them out of hand. He might carry a consuming hatred within him for the man who had stolen his birthright, but that was strictly a matter of honour. And what would a gentleman be without honour?

Richard decided he'd do much better to concentrate his energies on regaining his health. That he was at least mentally fit he proved that evening by thoroughly trouncing Edward in their first chess match. Edward retaliated with the second game. It was, possibly, unfair of Salford to introduce his cousin Lizzie's name during the match. Richard found his attention flagging, and Edward was swift to take advantage.

"Check and checkmate!" he crowed, removing Richard's queen and placing it in his sling with the pawns he had collected. "Now what were you asking about Lizzie? I assure you, Richard, you have nothing to fear. Once I explained why you couldn't keep your engagement, she was most understanding. As a matter of fact, I think she imagines you to be some sort of knight-errant."

"Knight-errant? Edward, what precisely did you tell your cousin?"

"Why, just that you bravely fended off three villainous footpads and saved her favourite cousin's life—at peril to your own."

"My God. I'll be embarrassed to face the girl."

"Nonsense. Thing is, though I trust you won't spread it about, Lizzie's a bit of a bluestocking. Always been one for sticking her nose in a book. She reads all that romantic drivel and she's got these notions of chivalry on her brain. Fact is, the average gentleman don't stand a chance with her."

Richard groaned. "If you had two good arms, I believe I'd strangle you. She'll be expecting me to perform some sort of heroic feat. What do you propose I do for an encore?"

"Not a thing, old man. Even a romantic like Lizzie won't expect you to do anything for a bit—not when you were fatally wounded."

"You never told her that! Edward, if I had been *fatally* wounded, I wouldn't be alive."

"And you practically weren't for two days. Now don't go splitting hairs. It can't hurt you to have a girl like Lizzie half in love with you."

Richard sobered, the laughter fleeing his face, and the crescent scar beneath his eye pulsated. "It can hurt a great deal when I'm not in a position to offer for her."

"Are we discussing your health, or something else? The on-dit is that you returned to England to find a wife."

"That's not entirely true. Can I trust you to keep a confidence?"

"I should call you out for that."

"My apologies. I believe the wine has addled my wits. The truth is I returned to England to avenge my father's death and reclaim my home. I can't think about Miss Fairchild, or any other lady, until I've settled my affairs."

Edward rose and poured them each another glass of wine, placing the decanter on the chess board between them. "I won't press you, Richard, if you don't wish to discuss this, but it sounds deuced serious. Care to tell me about it?"

Richard debated for a moment. Edward believed himself deeply indebted to him, and it was just possible that he might be of some help. There had been an instant rapport between the two young men, and Richard felt instinctively that he could trust this man. He'd confide in him—up to a point.

"I lived in Yorkshire as a boy, in an old rambling house that had been in my family for generations. You know the sort of place—large, drafty rooms, cold in the winter and damp in the summer. But I loved it all the same. I used to ride over the estate, and I think I knew every blade of grass on it. I don't know if you can understand how I felt, but it was like a part of me."

Edward nodded. He, too, had grown up on a beloved country estate. Although his love had been tempered by the knowledge that it would be George, his older brother, who would one day inherit it.

Richard continued, "It wasn't until I was eight or nine that I began to realize there was trouble at home. My parents quarrelled frequently, and my father would disappear for days at a time. My mother...seemed to cry a great deal, and kept more and more to her rooms. I was uneasy, and I suppose I avoided the house as much as I could."

Richard slowly rose and tentatively took a few steps. He seldom spoke of his childhood, and he was finding it harder than he'd anticipated. "One afternoon, I came home and found my belongings packed. My father had disappeared again, and Mother told me that they thought I would be better off, at least for a time, with her cousin Josiah—in India. He was a wealthy man, even then. And the only one of Mother's relations that my father tolerated."

Edward didn't know what to say. His own boyhood had been relatively carefree, and he silently offered his friend a cigar.

Richard waved it away, anxious now to finish his story. "My mother told me things were a bit difficult, financially. She had written to her cousin and asked him to invite me for a visit. The last thing I remember about her was her hugging me and telling me how much she loved me. I found it...difficult to believe when she was so willing to send me away."

"Know what you mean," Edward offered. "Mine keeps threatening to send me North—for my own good, of course."

His remark eased the tension and Richard returned to his chair, stretching out his legs. "I realize, now, that she meant it for the best, but at the time it seemed like a betrayal. I wouldn't even say goodbye to her, and though she wrote me a few times, I refused to read or answer her letters." He sighed. "I don't mean for it to sound as if I had a deprived childhood. I didn't. Josiah Danvers treated me like a favoured son. He took me everywhere with him. He bought me clothes, boots, horses, anything I wished for. Provided me with the best of tutors...and all I could do was talk about going home."

Edward nodded. "Some things never change. Here we put you in the best room, feed you well, give you excellent company, and all you do is talk about going home. I'm glad to know it's not just me. I fancy there's more to this tale. Go on."

"I was about twelve when a letter came from Father. I remember how excited I was, certain he was summoning me home. I almost tore it apart in my haste to open it. My father wrote that he had to sell off some of our land. He'd been cheated by a neighbour who had been scheming for years to take over our estate. It was a bitter letter, full of Father's misfortunes and his hatred for his neighbour...and at the very end...just a brief line or two to tell me my mother had died."

"Good God. How horrible for you. Did your cousin send you home?"

"No...Father didn't want me to come, though he wrote frequently after that. His letters were always the same. With each one, he was closer to financial ruin, and I know he feared debtors' prison. Josiah sent him money after each correspondence, but it was never enough. The last letter came when I was eighteen. Father knew he was going to die. He wrote blindly, as if he couldn't control his thoughts. The letter rambled, and in places, didn't even make sense. He blamed his death on his neighbour, and several times pleaded with me to come home and avenge him."

"Was he serious? Do you mean there was foul play?"

"My father was certain of it. In all his letters he accused one man of cheating him, stealing his lands and plotting to destroy him. I was contacted by a solicitor's firm a few days later. They informed me that my father had taken his own life. What was left of the estate would be sold to pay off his debts. The only thing left to me was the house itself, which is probably a ruin by now, and the few acres surrounding it. Josiah did what he could. He wrote the solicitors at once and offered to buy up the property. It was too late, however—everything now belonged to one man—the same neighbour my father had accused of scheming the take-over all along.''

"This is simply unbelievable. What did you do?"

"Nothing, I'm afraid. Oh, I was ready to come home. And young and foolish enough to take on an army. But Josiah stopped me. His health had been failing, and I had assumed more and more of the responsibilities of running his company. He begged me to stay. I was his heir, and he reminded me that when he died, I'd be a wealthy man. Then, he said, I could do as I pleased. Josiah was all the family I had left, and he'd been good to me." Richard lifted his hands in a gesture of helplessness.

Edward reached for the decanter. "I think we could use a little more wine. So you stayed. And now?"

"That was seven years ago. Josiah died last winter. But even at the end, he didn't want me to leave. He talked a lot about my father. Said he'd been a sick man, consumed by hatred. And then he mentioned my mother. I hadn't thought about her much, but he made me promise to always remember that she had loved me dearly. He said he owed her that, and he hoped one day she would forgive him. Well, anyway, I laid my plans and here I am. Funny, my father always said his neighbour had knifed him in the back figuratively. Who would have thought that my first week in London, I'd be knifed in the back literally?" He gave Edward a lopsided grin and lifted his glass. "Like Father, like son."

CHAPTER FOUR

THE WEEKEND passed pleasantly, and late on Monday afternoon Richard was pronounced well enough to return home. He received the news jubilantly, although the doctor warned him it would be some months before he would regain full use of his shoulder.

"No need to worry about him, Halymont," Lord Edward said, placing his own good arm round Richard's shoulders. "I intend to keep a close eye on him. I'll make certain he doesn't come to any harm."

"How reassuring, Lord Edward. I can only wonder that the thought doesn't fill me with confidence." And with a pointed look at Edward's injury, the doctor added, "You just keep your own arm in that sling, and give it time to heal properly before trying any more of your rum rigs."

Edward looked affronted, but Richard only laughed. "We certainly look as though we need someone to watch over us." He extended his left hand. "Thank you, sir, for your excellent care."

Before the gentlemen could escort Halymont out, a footman tapped on the door and informed them that the duchess wished their presence in the Yellow Drawing-room. They took their leave of the doctor, and walked down the hall, speculating on why the duchess wished to see them.

"Probably morning callers Mama wants us to make our bow to," Edward groaned. "She never tires of introducing me to all the eligible young ladies who call."

"But why should she include me?"

"And why not? She thinks very highly of you, Richard. Has some notion that you're a steadying influence."

"Of which you obviously stand in need."

Edward had no chance to retort. A footman, in blue-and-gold livery, opened the doors to the drawingroom, and announced them.

Richard's eyes were drawn at once to Elizabeth Fairchild, seated next to the duchess. She looked like liquid sunshine, he thought, with her blond hair piled in curls, and a bright yellow ribbon laced through them. The same colour ribbon was used to accent the high waist and long sleeves of her white muslin day dress.

The duchess rose at once. "Here are our wounded gallants, now. Mr. Danvers, my guests were quite concerned over the rumours abounding in Town regarding your injury. Miss Fairchild tells me one report had you at death's door. And her aunt, Mrs. Davenport, insisted on seeing for herself that you had quite recovered."

Richard bowed and addressed the aunt. "It was extraordinarily kind of you, ma'am, to concern yourself."

"Kindness had nothing to say to the matter. I am merely indulging in vulgar curiosity. I wished to see for myself the young man capable of performing heroic deeds, as Edward assured us you did."

"Aunt Horatia!"

"Hush, child. One of the few advantages granted to the aged is the privilege of saying what one pleases. And heaven knows there are few enough compensations for growing old and wrinkled. Now young man—Danvers,

is it? You're the one who was supposed to come to tea.
Let me have another look at you.''

Richard struggled to hide a smile as the old lady put a
quizzing glass to her eye, and boldly looked him up and
down. Roscoe had brought him clean clothes, and he was
confident that he looked quite presentable in a green cut-
away coat and white knee breeches. His stock was only of
moderate height, and his green-and-white striped waistcoat fitted perfectly.

''Well, you don't look like a member of the ton. Perhaps that accounts for it.''

''I beg your pardon?'' he said, eyebrows rising a notch.

''Don't be offended, young man. I am paying you a
compliment. The so-called *gentlemen* I've seen this Season are such glorified creatures that they put the ladies to
shame. And not an ounce of gumption among them. Too
much inbreeding, no doubt. The ton needs new blood.''

Elizabeth tried to pretend she was unconscious of her
aunt's words, while Edward coughed to hide his laughter. Richard decided Mrs. Davenport had a great deal in
common with his late stepfather. Josiah always spoke in
just such a blunt, forthright manner. Imagining the two
of them together caused Richard to grin at her impu-
dently.

The duchess, accustomed to Horatia's outspokenness,
calmly poured out tea for the gentlemen and remarked
quietly, ''I don't believe that Mr. Danvers has any reason to blush for his breeding.''

''I did not say he did. Only that he doesn't look like
this year's crop of young dandies with their padded
shoulders and legs and neckcloths so high they can't turn
their heads. He looks like a man, and I should not be at
all averse if he chose to pay Elizabeth court.'' She beamed
at Richard. ''I wish I could recall who it is you put me in

mind of. One of the old-line families, I'm sure. Well, never mind. I'll remember eventually. You bring yourself to tea tomorrow, and we'll discuss it.''

"Thank you, Mrs. Davenport, I should be delighted.''

"Elizabeth, take Mr. Danvers and your cousin out to the rose garden. I wish a few words with Her Grace."

Elizabeth had little choice. She rose gracefully, and hardly daring to look at Richard, murmured softly, "Have you seen the garden, sir? The duchess is renowned for her extraordinary roses."

The trio passed through the French doors leading to the informal garden. The roses were blooming profusely, and Elizabeth had a chance to regain her composure as she pointed out the different varieties. "I've never seen roses do as well as they do here. We have a small rose garden at home, but it can't compare with this."

Richard snapped a yellow rose and presented it to her. Its creamy centre reminded him of her delicate complexion. "I suggest you apply to Mrs. Chambers for some of her special broth. Dr. Halymont told me that your cousin and his brother have been feeding it to the rosebushes for years."

Edward laughed aloud. "I didn't think the old sawbones knew. Well, it wouldn't do to offend Nanna, and it certainly hasn't hurt the roses."

Elizabeth couldn't resist teasing him. "But Edward, only think what a magnificent specimen you could've been had you eaten the broth. Why, I'll wager a bowl of Nanna's broth once a week and you could equal Mr. Danvers in appearance—"

Edward pulled one of her curls. "And you, Lizzie, should have some as well. It might add a few more inches to your stature, and then you wouldn't be such a dab of a girl."

"Well, I like that. I'll have you know that even Lord Muscrief said I was a diamond of the first water."

"That old court-card? Don't tell me he's one of your admirers!"

"I fear so," Elizabeth sighed. "Mama has been encouraging him, and she never loses an opportunity to point out all his advantages."

"You can't be serious. Why, he's three times your age, and can barely walk."

"I wish you would tell Mama how ludicrous it is. All she can see is the title and his fortune."

"I shouldn't worry, Lizzie. Your great-aunt would never permit such a match for you."

"No. Aunt Horatia told me after our first evening at Almack's that she would be content to see me a spinster rather than wed to any of the ninny-hammers passing themselves off as gentlemen." Her mimicry of her aunt was perfect and the trio laughed.

"Obviously the lady has very high standards," Richard said, preening himself, and hoping to make her laugh again. He liked the way her eyes lit up when she was amused, and the high cheekbones seemed to become more rounded when she smiled. He found himself more than a little envious of the special closeness she and Edward seemed to share. He had never known that kind of relationship.

Elizabeth rewarded him with a smile, a becoming flush of colour tinting her cheeks. "I am sorry if my great-aunt embarrassed you, Mr. Danvers. Please don't feel that you have to... to..."

"To pay you court?" he teased. "My intellect may not be high, Miss Fairchild, but I would think myself extremely stupid to take offence where none was intended, and to deny myself the very great pleasure of your company as well."

"Very pretty," Edward said approvingly. "I didn't know you had such address. But if you mean to cut me out with all the ladies, then I don't think I shall thank you for saving my life."

"Since it's a bag of moonshine, there's no need. Miss Fairchild, did you know your cousin is prone to exaggeration? He insists on telling everyone that I saved his life when it was quite the other way round."

"Lizzie, do take note of the becoming air of modesty. I think Great-Aunt would approve, don't you?"

"Very definitely. When you call tomorrow, Mr. Danvers, you must strike just that note of humbleness. It will impress Aunt Horatia."

"The next thing you know, your great-aunt will be expecting me to come charging up on a white stallion and carry you off to my castle."

"She does admire a man with a good seat," Elizabeth teased. "But the castle might prove a problem. You don't just happen to own one, do you, Mr. Danvers?"

"Not a castle, precisely. More of an Abbey that is undoubtedly in ruins, and the few acres it stands on. However, it's been in my family for generations, and I hope to restore it."

"Richard, dear boy!" a soft voice trilled from the terrace.

The trio turned to see a striking young lady in a dark blue gown and bonnet, standing just outside the French doors, waving merrily to Richard.

"Aren't you surprised to see me? When Her Grace told me you were here, I could not credit my ears."

She advanced the few yards to Richard's side and, taking his face between her gloved hands, kissed him soundly on each cheek. "This is utterly delightful. I had not looked for such a pleasure as seeing you again, my friend."

Richard, paling quite visibly, cursed his fate. But there was nothing of his dismay in his voice as he answered, "Lady Weymouth, this is a surprise. May I present Miss Fairchild, and Lord Edward Salford? My friends, this is Lady Victoria Weymouth. We were acquainted in India."

"Acquainted? Fie on you, Richard." Victoria reached up and patted his cheek. "Why I considered us to be the *closest* of friends." Elizabeth had stepped aside with Edward, and Victoria lost no time hooking her arm in Richard's. After a brief look at the young girl, she remarked patronizingly, "Dear child, don't eat me. You must know that I almost married Richard. And had I known he would grow into such a handsome gentleman, I would have been even more tempted."

Elizabeth studied her, and didn't care for what she saw. Lady Weymouth might have a voluptuous figure, and luxuriously thick, black hair, but to Elizabeth she looked more like a courtesan than a lady. And, she thought spitefully, she's at least several years older than Mr. Danvers. Her eyes opened wide, and she looked sweetly innocent as she enquired, "And when was that, Lady Weymouth?"

Richard chose to answer for her. "Seven years ago."

"How dear of you to remember," Victoria purred.

"Why, you could hardly have been more than a boy," Elizabeth pointed out, managing to sound surprised.

Richard pulled at his neckcloth, which was feeling unaccountably tight. "The air is growing considerably cooler. Perhaps we should rejoin your great-aunt?"

Elizabeth, half-hoping he would gainsay her, replied, "Edward will see me in, sir. I'm certain Lady Weymouth desires a few words with you in private. Pray, excuse us."

"How discerning of the child." Victoria smiled. "Come, Richard, sit on the bench with me and tell me how you come to be in England. I thought you fixed with Josiah for ever."

Richard made no move to sit beside her. For a few brief seconds, Elizabeth had looked like a favoured spaniel whose master had abused it. He longed to go after her, and his reply to the lady was curt.

"Josiah died a few months ago. I really must go in, Lady Weymouth. I'm recovering from a shoulder wound and I fear the chill in the air does me no good."

Deep violet eyes, heavily lashed, fluttered at him. The lips that Richard had once declared were created solely to be kissed, formed a pretty pout. "Lady Weymouth sounds so formal. You used to call me Victorie."

"That, my lady, was before you were wed." His words were cold, but he couldn't prevent his eyes from straying to the revealing cut of her gown. Creamy breasts were exposed by the low decolletage, and he remembered how he could span her waist with his hands. Ashamed of his thoughts, he extended his hand. "Shall we join the others?"

She stood reluctantly, placing her hand possessively on his arm. "Only if you insist, my dear Richard. However, I warn you, I mean to see something of you while we are in London. I've thought of you so often, *mon cher*. Did you never think of me?"

Richard didn't answer. He held open the door for her, and Victoria gave him an arch smile as she swept into the room. Lord Weymouth hurried over and took his wife's arm with a proprietary air.

Victoria patted his hand. "Look, darling, I found an old friend. You remember Richard Danvers, don't you?"

Weymouth was a portly man with a cherubic face. He beamed at Richard. "Course I remember him. You're the young sprig I cut out with Vicky. Hope you've forgiven me by now. All's fair in love and war, what?"

"Of course, sir. Will you excuse me? I see Mrs. Davenport and Miss Fairchild are leaving."

Elizabeth had hoped to be gone by the time Richard Danvers returned. Aunt Horatia, however, had recollected a bit of scandalous gossip about a mutual friend and was determined to find out the truth of the matter from the duchess. Elizabeth, trying to concentrate on what the duchess was saying, saw Richard cross the room. She was all too aware when he stood directly behind her. And though she willed herself not to look, she couldn't close her ears to his soft voice.

"I'm sorry you're leaving so soon, Miss Fairchild. We've barely had a chance to talk."

Elizabeth turned, feigning surprise. "Oh, Mr. Danvers. I quite thought you'd be preoccupied for some time. It's so pleasant to renew old friendships, is it not?"

"Not nearly so pleasurable as pursuing new ones."

"How unchivalrous of you, sir," she chided, but her voice had regained its lilt, and the look in her eyes said his words pleased her.

"I'm looking forward to tea tomorrow. Edward gave me your direction, and I shall present myself promptly at four."

"Until tomorrow, then." She extended her hand, and Richard executed a graceful bow. Mrs. Davenport nodded approvingly, and as the ladies left, her voice carried back down the hall. "I like the cut of him, Elizabeth. Reminds me of someone. Now who is it?"

Richard returned to the group gathered round the fireplace. Victoria, sitting demurely by her husband's side, appeared engrossed in his conversation. Lord Weymouth was holding forth on the deplorable state of the roads, and patiently explaining to Lord Edward how lax the turnpike authorities had become.

The duchess, a consummate hostess, tried to draw Richard into their circle. "Mr. Danvers, Lord and Lady Weymouth were telling me they had the pleasure of your acquaintance in India. It must be wonderful for you to find familiar faces here."

"Indeed, Your Grace."

Victoria flashed him a smile. "Shall you be in Town for long, Richard? William and I are here for a fortnight. Of course, William will be closeted with the duke for much of the time." The remark was hardly subtle, and Richard didn't doubt her broad hint was clear to everyone.

"You mustn't feel you'll be neglected, Lady Weymouth," the duchess interceded smoothly. "We have several other guests arriving later today. Lord and Lady Coltraine will be here, Lord Frome, the Marquis of Bromwich, and the Countess of Wrexham. Others will be arriving during the week. And I do assure you, we have numerous entertainments planned for your amusement. I'm certain you'll enjoy meeting the countess."

"Thank you, Your Grace. It sounds quite wonderful. But actually, I am already acquainted with the countess." She turned to Richard again. "You remember her, don't you? She made quite a sensation at that dinner your stepfather gave for Lord Minto.''

Richard nodded curtly. His face had grown hard, and the tiny scar beneath his right eye pulsed rapidly. Victoria stared at him, puzzled. Richard stood abruptly.

"I must beg to be excused, Your Grace, and complete my packing.''

"Of course, Mr. Danvers, if you are certain I cannot persuade you to extend your stay?''

"Thank you, but I feel I've imposed on you for too long as it is.''

"Nonsense. We owe you a debt I can never repay, and it is not an obligation I shall readily forget. You may leave now, sir, but I shall expect to see you frequently in the future.''

Richard smiled and bowed over her hand. Of Lord and Lady Weymouth, he took a polite leave, and was about to shake hands with Lord Edward. His friend, however, begged leave as well, and walked with Richard back to his room. "I hadn't realized you moved in such exalted company, Richard. The countess, no less. And Lord Minto. Who else did your stepfather invite to dinner?''

Richard smiled. "I didn't mean to give you a false impression of my stepfather. He settled in Calcutta a few years before Charles Cornwallis was made Governor General. Josiah served in the East India Company long enough to learn his way round, and he was a Senior Merchant when he retired. Cornwallis valued his knowledge and they became good friends. I think the Governor General used his influence on Josiah's behalf, and I know my stepfather did everything he could to help Cornwallis, which included a good deal of entertaining. The English in Calcutta are a close-knit group—especially after the Black Hole incident. Josiah frequently had the Governor to the house for dinner. And where the Governor went, the rest followed. The countess was a frequent visitor, and a favourite of Josiah's. He liked to argue politics with her.''

"Then obviously," Edward said, watching him, "it wasn't mention of the countess that brought that cold look to your eyes when Mother was reeling off the guest list."

"You're far too observant by half, my friend. You must guard that long nose of yours doesn't get you into trouble."

"I thought we were friends, but if you feel you can't trust me..." He shrugged.

"Of course I trust you. It's only..." Richard paused and took a deep breath. "The duchess mentioned Lord Frome. When I was still living at home, I overheard a dreadful quarrel between my parents. I didn't understand it at the time, but apparently Father believed my mother was having an affair with Lord Frome."

"I don't believe it!"

"I did not ask you to. You insisted on knowing, however."

"But Lord Frome? Have you ever met him? Richard, he's one of the most honourable men I know. There's never been a breath of scandal about him."

"It's old gossip, in any event. It would've been fifteen or sixteen years ago. It might not even be the same man."

Edward deemed it was time to change the subject, and after a few minutes of silence, he drawled, "I can see that befriending you is not going to be as simple as I had thought."

Richard glanced up. "Now, how am I supposed to take that?''

"As a warning. If you are going to cut me out with all the most attractive ladies, I shall have to drop you. Nothing else for it. You'll ruin my reputation."

"That's the second time you've said that. Soon, I shall think you are serious. The truth is, I'm not much of a hand with the ladies."

"Hmm. First it was Lizzie. She's very taken with you, Richard. That's why her nose was a trifle out of joint when Lady Weymouth arrived. And that rather beautiful lady also seems—"

"Lady Weymouth means nothing to me. I had a boyhood infatuation with her when I was eighteen. That's all."

"Well, it looked to me, and doubtless to Lizzie, as if the lady would be delighted to pick up where you left off."

"She might be, but I promise you, I haven't any such inclination."

"Are you going to leave me hanging, or tell me what happened?"

"There's not a lot to tell. I was infatuated with her— the way only a young boy can be with his first love. I was rather shy with the ladies, and Victoria was the first woman to flatter me with her attention. I wanted to marry her, and I think she was seriously considering my offer, when Weymouth appeared on the scene. He had a fortune and a title. Victoria never hesitated."

"As heartless as she is beautiful?"

"I thought so at the time, certainly. Now I don't know. She's the daughter of a parson. Good family, but her father was a younger son. Victoria grew up in the shadow of her wealthy cousins, and from things she told me, I gather they made her feel rather inferior. Money and position were important to her. I suppose the idea of becoming Lady Weymouth was just too overwhelming a temptation."

"It wouldn't have been if she'd truly loved you. I think you should count yourself fortunate that she chose Weymouth."

"I do. Josiah always said I would. Of course it was his doing that Lord Weymouth was on the scene at just the right time. I really don't have any regrets—not now. She left India immediately after her betrothal was announced, and I never thought to see her again. But, Edward, if you think she's beautiful now, you should have seen her seven years ago."

"I can imagine. She must have been ravishing."

"An understatement. I was flattered beyond belief, and devastated when she chose Weymouth. I believe I even swore off women forever."

His friend laughed, as Richard had intended, although there was an element of truth in his words. Victoria had been the first female he had cared for, aside from his mother. And that both women had betrayed him had hurt him more deeply than he would admit.

Roscoe burst into the room, and halted abruptly. "Beggin' your pardon, sir. I didn't realize as how you were here with his lordship."

"It's all right, Roscoe. I'm just gathering up the last of my things. Have Kirby bring the carriage round."

"He's already waiting out front, sir. Here, let me do that." Roscoe took the shirt Richard was attempting to fold and packed it neatly.

Edward rose and held out his hand. "I know it's useless to try to persuade you to stay longer, so I'll say goodbye for now. Shall I call for you later this evening? It's time I introduced you to White's. We'll dine first, and then visit my club, if that's agreeable?"

Richard allowed that it was, and the gentlemen settled on a time while Roscoe moved impatiently about the room. As soon as the door shut behind Lord Edward, he urged Richard to hurry along.

"What's your rush, Roscoe? Is someone after you? I haven't seen you bustle about so fast in a score of years. We've plenty of time."

"It's Kirby, sir. The horses have been standing a good while, and are on the fret. He knows how you hate to keep your horses standing. Here, let me help you into your coat, sir."

"Your concern for my horses does you credit, Roscoe, but who ordered the carriage brought round so soon?" He allowed the valet to smooth the coat over his shoulder, and when the little man didn't reply, he strolled over to a mahogany dressing mirror. Adjusting the tilt of the mirror so he could watch Roscoe's reaction, he asked with a smile, "All this unseemly haste wouldn't have anything to do with the fact that Lord and Lady Weymouth arrived here this morning, would it?"

Dismay and helplessness warred on the valet's face. He was no longer in a hurry to leave, and stood as if frozen, staring at this master. "You've seen her, then?"

"Afraid so, old man. Lord Edward and I were in the drawing room when she arrived. And there's no need for that voice of doom. Her husband travels with her."

Roscoe snorted. "For all she might be a titled lady now, she don't behave like Quality. To one like her, a husband is only a licence to—"

"Roscoe! Now that's enough. You have no reason to slander the lady."

"No?" With a challenging look, the valet removed a crumpled billet from his pocket and proffered it to Richard. "You jest tell me what kind of lady sends perfumed notes like this behind her husband's back."

Richard stared at the envelope, loath to touch it. He could smell Victoria's scent of violets. "Where did you get this?"

"She caught me in the hall, and told me to make sure I give it to you—in private."

Richard reluctantly took the note from his hand. "I suppose if you had managed to get me out of here without knowing of her arrival, you would have forgotten to give me this?"

Roscoe avoided his eyes and stood silent.

"Take the bags down and wait with Kirby. I'll be along directly."

When he was alone in the room, Richard sat down and stared at the note for several minutes. He glanced at the fireplace, half-tempted to toss the note in, unread. Finally deciding that he owed it to Victoria to at least read the note, he slit the envelope.

Richard, mon cher,
It is urgent that I have an opportunity to speak with you privately. Meet me in Hyde Park tomorrow at three. I am in desperate trouble, and you are the only friend I have in England. Please don't fail me.

Victorie.

CHAPTER FIVE

BOTH EDWARD AND RICHARD were in high spirits when they descended from their carriage in St. James's Street shortly before nine that evening. Although it was unfashionably early to be visiting White's, Lord Edward wished his friend to see the rooms before they became overly crowded and dense with cigar smoke.

Richard, while suitably impressed with the size and elegance of the subscription room, the card rooms and the more than ample dining facilities, was not even a little awed when Lord Edward pointed out to him the infamous bow window.

It was too early for Brummel to be present, of course, but Lord Worcester, John Mills, and Lord de Ros were seated, and even as they watched, Lord Sefton joined the inner circle.

"Those gentlemen are the arbiters of all London fashion," Edward whispered, a trifle awed. "A word from them and you could set a new style, or else become a laughingstock overnight."

"And have they nothing better to do than watch London parade by their window?"

Lord Edward hastily drew Richard away before it chanced they were overheard. "I don't believe you understand, Richard. The gentlemen privileged to sit in that window are the élite of London Society. They are practically all members of the Four-Horse Club, and several of them sit in the House of Lords. And Brummel, of course, is frequently consulted by the Prince Regent."

"From what I've heard of our precious Regent, that is hardly a recommendation. He is not at all well thought of in India." At Edward's look of astonishment, Richard added, "Forgive my rudeness, my friend. It's merely that it's difficult for me to conceive of living a life of such idleness. I suppose my upbringing has ill prepared me to be a gentleman of leisure. I had a great deal of responsibility in overseeing my stepfather's affairs."

"Naturally, and I quite understand, but do not, I beg of you, utter such sentiments to anyone else here. Now come along, and allow me to introduce you to some of the other members."

Lord Edward, with no more than a regretful glance at the dice table, led Richard through to a card room. Their progress was slow as numerous acquaintances commiserated with Salford on his arm and, on learning Richard's identity, applauded him for his bravery. Richard's head was swimming with new names and faces when they finally reached the corner table where Admiral Trafalgar and Lord Demeral were playing whist.

Edward introduced him to both the older men, and although Demeral remained seated, the admiral rose and extended his hand. His vast stomach strained the seams of his waistcoat, and Richard felt almost dwarfed by his massive height. Trafalgar might have been getting on in years, but his handshake was still strong, and his voice boomed above the noise in the room.

"Danvers, is it? I knew a Josiah Danvers once. Are you any kin?"

"Why yes, sir. Josiah was my stepfather."

"Was?"

Richard nodded. "I regret to tell you that he died last year."

Shaking his head, Trafalgar indicated they should all be seated. "I'm truly sorry to hear that, laddie. Old Danvers did me a good turn once—it's a debt I never had the chance to repay. Lord, it's hard to believe he's gone. I thought he'd live forever. What happened to his company?"

"He left it to me, sir. I've been managing his affairs for several years."

Trafalgar's face split into a wide grin, and he nudged Demeral. "Up the stakes. Danvers here must be worth a king's ransom."

Lord Demeral, playing whist with the admiral only because he could ill afford the higher stakes at other tables, warned Richard, "I'm living proof, Mr. Danvers, that wealth can be a fleeting illusion. I'd advise you to guard yours carefully within these portals."

Edward laughed, believing the warning was intended for him as well as Richard, and excused himself to see about drinks for the table.

Richard, however, studied the older man. He judged Demeral's hair must have once been as black as his beard, though it was now liberally streaked with grey. Bushy brows arched slightly above small, calculating eyes deep set above a long, narrow nose. His lips were thin and narrow, devoid of all colour, and when he opened his mouth, yellow teeth showed unpleasantly. Demeral was half smiling, and Richard wondered that anyone could be so sanguine about losing a fortune. He half-suspected the man of roasting him and reproached him, "If you indeed lost your wealth here, I confess I'm surprised you still frequent the place."

"Fortunes are won and lost here every day, Mr. Danvers, on the turn of a card, or the throw of the dice. I assure you my situation is not at all unusual. I could name you a dozen gentlemen who have suffered the same fate, and a score more if I stopped to think about it."

"I'm still astonished, sir, that you continue to play."

"How else do I recoup my losses? One day Dame Fortune will turn her smile on me. Then, perhaps, I can buy my estates back from Lord Pembroke."

Richard froze. The scar beneath his eye turned white and pulsed rapidly. He took a deep breath and tried to speak calmly. "My father once mentioned a Lord Pembroke. Rowland Pembroke, I believe. Would that be the same gentleman? Is he a member of White's?"

Demeral nodded. "But you'll not see him here. Pembroke retired from Society. It's been years since anyone has seen the old reprobate."

"Now, Demeral, you know it was your own foolishness which lost you that game," the admiral admonished. "Let's not be raking up ancient history. Ah, here's Lord Edward."

Edward was closely followed by Dakins, who took their orders for drinks, and the four finally settled down to the cards. The gentlemen seemed evenly matched, but Lord Edward played carelessly, and Richard deliberately underplayed his hand. Lord Demeral might hold the key to his learning more about Pembroke. If losing fifty pounds to the man would incur his favour, Richard counted the loss well worth it.

It was nearly midnight when Edward threw down his cards in disgust. "Enough! I couldn't win this evening if the cards were marked for me."

"Just as well you lost, Lord Edward," Trafalgar jostled him. "With that sling on your arm, someone would be certain to accuse you of concealing cards had you won."

"Surely not in a gentleman's club," Richard said, rising.

"As likely here as anywhere, I fear," the admiral said, giving Edward a large wink. "Isn't that right, Demeral?"

"There have been *accusations*," his lordship sneered. "But that's only to be expected when you have so many young cubs playing too deep. Then when they lose what they can ill afford, they're quick to declare someone cheated them." His words were sharp, and he directed a venomous look at the admiral before adding, "And most of the disputes end up being settled on the dueling field."

"If you're thinking of calling me out, think again," Trafalgar laughed. "I'm too old for such nonsense, and I didn't mean to offend you, Demeral. You're too prickly by half. I don't know why I put up with you."

"Or I with you." Lord Demeral bowed, but the tension had eased and he smiled affably at Edward and Richard. "It's been a pleasure, gentlemen."

Richard allowed Edward to stroll ahead with the admiral, while he spoke quietly to Demeral. "I would like to talk with you further, Lord Demeral. I believe we may have much in common. Would you do me the honour of dining with me, say, next Tuesday? And after dinner, perhaps we might have another game. You owe me the chance to recover my losses."

Lord Demeral was quick to agree. He saw before him a pigeon ripe for the plucking. The forty pounds he had taken from Danvers had been a godsend. Tuesday, he said, was quite agreeable, and after obtaining Richard's direction, the two men shook hands.

Lord Edward watched them from the doorway, and for a brief moment, a frown marred his usually amiable features. His brow cleared, however, as Richard joined him, and he was determined to say nothing until they were settled in his carriage. Even then, Edward hesitated. Of all things, what he most loathed was unsolicited advice from well-meaning friends.

Richard watched him, amusement crinkling the corners of his eyes and turning up his mouth in a wry smile. "Out with it, Edward. You're bursting to tell me something, and we're too good of friends for you to have to pick your words. Whatever it is you're worrying over, I promise you I won't take offence."

Edward sighed. "I hate to blacken a man's reputation without any proof, and yet, I can't allow you to engage Demeral in a private game without warning you, either."

"I rather thought it might have something to do with my invitation to Demeral. Are you worried I shall lose my fortune to him? You needn't be."

"I know you're capable of playing more skillfully than you did this evening. But Demeral has been, shall we say, suspected of cheating. That's what Trafalgar was alluding to earlier. Nothing was ever proved, you understand. Demeral would call anyone out who dared to point a finger, and as he's a deadly shot, well, one hesitates."

"And yet you chose to play with the man this evening."

"Only because of the admiral. Friend of my father's. And Demeral's not likely to fuzz the cards at White's. No, he saves that sort of thing for private games—where there's no one to witness it, should he be caught out."

"You alarm me, Edward."

"Oddly enough, you don't look in the least alarmed. Now dash it, Richard, stop laughing. You must take this seriously."

The carriage slowed to a stop in front of Richard's townhouse. As he opened the door, Richard grinned at his friend. "I am perfectly serious, Edward. And I do appreciate your concern. But you see, there's no need. I invited Demeral with the intention of losing to him, whether he cheats or no."

"I say Richard, you don't look badly foxed, but—"

"I'm not," he said, climbing down and closing the door. Richard took a step back from the carriage and gave a nod to the groom. With a salute to Edward, he called out, "We'll talk about it tomorrow." He couldn't help the laughter that escaped him at Edward's ludicrous expression. He was still laughing when he strolled inside. Although Philbin stood majestically in the hall, it was Roscoe who opened the door for him.

His valet plagued him with questions as they climbed the stairs, but Richard discreetly waited until they were within his room before telling him about Lord Demeral.

Concluding his tale, and lounging back in the chair, he allowed Roscoe to pull off his boots. "I suspect that with a few bottles of good wine, Demeral will talk rather freely."

"So your pa ain't the only one Lord Pembroke choused?"

"It would appear so. What surprises me is that Demeral is nobody's fool. It's difficult for me to imagine him being reckless enough to risk his entire fortune. But apparently he did."

"Didn't you say it was years ago? He might have been just a green boy at the time."

"Possibly, but Josiah would say tigers don't change their stripes. I don't believe Lord Demeral, even a very young Demeral, would have risked all without a decided edge."

Roscoe eased him out of his shirt, surreptitiously checking the shoulder bandage for signs of bleeding. "Well, if your pa was only half as knowing as you, then I figure this Pembroke must be pretty clever."

Richard stretched out on the bed, allowing Roscoe to change the bandage. He kept his thoughts to himself. His father's weakness for the bottle was something he had never understood and disliked discussing. It seemed disloyal, somehow, to even think that Lord. St. Symington's fondness for drink might have contributed to the loss of the Abbey. Richard pushed the thought away, concentrating on Lord Pembroke. *He* was responsible for his father's losing their lands, and apparently, for Demeral's loss, as well.

Roscoe, finished with the bandaging, helped Richard into his nightshirt and prepared to withdraw. He paused at the door and reminded his master, "Don't be forgetting, sir, that you're promised to Miss Fairchild tomorrow."

"I won't," Richard said, looking up in surprise, but his valet was half out the door. He wondered briefly what his man was about. Roscoe had certainly disapproved of his seeing Miss Fairchild, so why was he at pains now to remind Richard of the appointment? His injury and subsequent tendency to tire, however, had taken their toll. His mind wrestled with the problem for only a moment before sleep claimed him.

Nor did Richard have time to dwell on his personal problems the next morning. There were several urgent matters pertaining to his business in India that required his attention, and he was closeted in the library for several hours. Although he had left Bartholomew and Jamison in charge, both capable men, there were still decisions that only he was authorized to make. The delay involved before action could be taken greatly concerned Richard, and could prove costly to the company. He was debating, again, the wisdom of selling the business outright when Philbin announced Lord Edward.

Salford strolled in, looking cheerful and decidedly elegant. He tossed his beaver hat and cane onto a chair, and then looked aghast at the litter of papers spread over the large desk. "Richard! I thought to find you still abed, but judging from the look of things, you must have been up for hours."

"My lamentable upbringing again. Josiah and I normally spent the morning hours reviewing business affairs. It's a habit I find difficult to break."

"Commendable, I'm sure," Edward said, eyeing the papers again with a look of comical dismay. "But you mustn't forget that Halymont warned us both to get plenty of rest. We're still convalescents, you know."

"I suggest that you have a seat then, instead of standing there taxing your strength." Richard waved towards a chair, and rang for a footman. He knew Edward would prefer tea to the strong coffee which he and Josiah had grown accustomed to drinking. "Have you any plans for the afternoon, Edward? If not, I would appreciate your company."

"I'm entirely at your disposal. Where are we going?"

"First, to the Park, where I'm perfectly sure that I shall have need of you. And then to your cousin's for tea. That is, if you don't think the great-aunt will object to an uninvited guest?"

"No fear of that. The old girl will be pleased enough to see me. She enjoys grilling me. Thinks it's past time I was leg-shackled. But why the Park?"

Richard made a face. "An assignation. I hope your presence will act as a restraint to the lady involved."

Edward stood up. "Dash it all, Richard, it's not at all the thing. You can't accept an assignation and then bring along a chaperon. The lady will be wishing me to the devil." He paused, but couldn't resist adding, "Is she anyone I know?"

"Lady Weymouth."

"Lord, Richard, talk about awkward. If you don't wish to see her alone, can't you just cry off?"

"I considered it, of course. But Victoria sent me a billet saying the matter was urgent, and begged me not to fail her." He spread his hands in a helpless gesture. "It may be nothing, of course, but if it *is* important—if she's in some sort of trouble..."

"Very well, then, here's what we'll do. We take my carriage. When we come up with the lady, suggest a stroll. I'll keep you in sight, but at least she may say what she wishes in some sort of privacy. Then, if this is just a charade to be alone with you, reach up and adjust your hat. That shall be my signal to join you at once."

Richard agreed. Reluctantly. He knew Victoria would be incensed that he had not come alone, and dragging Edward into the affair was an act of cowardice. He recalled boasting to Roscoe that he was no longer a green boy, and would not be so easily ensnared by Victoria's wiles. He was no longer so certain of that. Lady Weymouth was incredibly beautiful, and had a way of looking at him that stirred his senses.

The two gentlemen set out for the Park shortly before the appointed hour. Edward, at least, was thankful that the lady had chosen an hour when the grounds were not terribly crowded. They passed only one carriage, and a group of strolling couples. "Where are you supposed to meet?"

"She didn't specify. I guess we just drive through and watch for her. I don't even know if she'll be walking or driving. She can tool a phaeton expertly, but I don't know if she has one at her disposal."

They had driven through the Park in one complete circle without a sign of Lady Weymouth, when Edward caught sight of a carriage from his own stables. Findley was handling the reins, and a heavily veiled lady sat within. "That'll be her." Edward nodded and made to pull alongside the landau.

"Hello, Findley. Who's your passenger?"

"Lady Weymouth, sir."

"Now that's a coincidence. Mr. Danvers here is an old friend of hers. Do you want to get down Richard and say hello?"

Richard merely nodded, red with embarrassment. He feared Edward's play-acting for the groom's benefit was only making matters worse.

Lady Weymouth had the carriage door open and gestured for Richard to join her inside. "Mr. Danvers, what a delightful surprise. Do take a turn about the Park with me."

"I doubt that would be wise," Richard whispered. He was all too aware of the groom's curiosity, although Edward was doing his best to engage him in conversation. Louder, he said, "Lady Weymouth, it's much too nice a day for a closed carriage. I suggest we stroll down one of these charming footpaths."

Victoria allowed him to assist her from the carriage. She judged, correctly, that it was the only way she could have private speech with him. The veil she wore hid the anger flashing in her eyes, while she inwardly cursed his prudence. Once Richard would have jumped at the opportunity to be alone with her, and hang the consequences.

Lord Edward greeted her with an embarrassed nod. "You two go on ahead. There's a matter I need to discuss with Findley."

Victoria hooked her arm in Richard's and the pair walked a short way along the footpath. Richard's nervous glances over his shoulder infuriated the lady, but there was nothing in her manner to indicate her displeasure. She leaned against Richard's left arm, her heavy scent enveloping them. "I am so pleased you found a way to meet with me, *mon cher.*"

"It was difficult, Lady Weymouth. As you can see, I had a prior engagement with Lord Edward, and we are both promised to...to someone else at four. However, as your note said it was urgent, I contrived as best I could."

"Thank you, dearest Richard. I declare I feel you're my only real friend in London, and I have been so dreadfully unhappy."

"Surely, Lady Weymouth, your husband should be the one—"

"Oh, pray, don't suggest I confide in him. *He* is the one making me so miserable. I was grossly deceived in him, Richard. The man is a positive beast."

"Really, Lady Weymouth, it would be better—"

"No. You do not know him, Richard. To the world he presents a jovial face, but in private he...abuses me. He does not care about me, only that I may influence this one or that one that he brings to the house. I am a possession to him, no more. Another acquisition to flaunt before his friends. I must escape, Richard. And you are the only one who can help me."

"Lady Weymouth, I—"

"Can you not call me Victorie as you used to do? I cannot believe you have forgotten all we once meant to each other." She turned to face him, lifting the veil from her face. Her large, dark eyes looked up at him, and she moistened her lips before parting them slightly.

Richard drew a ragged breath. Lord, she was beautiful. Her fingers were toying with the buttons on his waistcoat, and her eyes looked an invitation. He knew an insane impulse to sweep her into his arms. Only the sound of a carriage close by broke the spell.

Richard looked up, and although he couldn't identify the young ladies seated in the carriage, it was enough to recall him to his senses. His hand went to his hat, signalling Edward to rescue him. He captured Victoria's hands in his own, and tried to speak sensibly. "My dear Lady Weymouth, whatever might have passed between us once, ended with your marriage."

"But it was a mistake, Richard, a terrible mistake. It was not long before I realized that it was you that I truly loved." Tears glistened in her eyes, and Richard patted her shoulder helplessly.

"Please, Victoria, you mustn't say such things. Our situations have changed, and you owe your allegiance to your husband now."

"You do not listen! He is a beast! A vile person. I owe him nothing! I want only to escape from him. That's why I sent for you, *mon cher*. I must leave him, and I desperately need your help. Do not deny me, Richard."

"We cannot speak of this now. Lord Edward is coming. Let me help you back to your carriage."

Victoria went with him reluctantly. Eyes cast down, her mind was busy scheming. Ever since she'd learned from the duchess of Richard's vast wealth, she'd been determined to wed him. She had grown desperate and she feared that if Weymouth ever learned the truth about her, he'd cast her off without a pound to her name. Richard, who lived all those years in a more casual society, would be more likely to understand and forgive her. If she could convince him to return with her to India, he'd marry her in spite of the scandal it would cause. As it was, he was her only hope.

She looked up to see the same carriage circling again. Two young girls were staring in their direction. Victoria pretended to twist her ankle and fell heavily against Richard. Caught off guard, he managed to support her with his good arm. In pretended fright, she wound both her arms around his neck and smiled over his shoulder at the girls in the carriage. Edward ran the last few steps to help Richard, and between them, they got the lady back to her carriage. Edward instructed Findley to take her ladyship home at once.

"She was shamming it, Richard, I'm dammed certain of it."

"Very likely, but the damage is done. Did you see who was in that carriage?"

"Do you mean the Brookhurst girls?"

Richard nodded. "I'll wager ten to one the tale will be all over Town before this evening. And the Lord only knows what Victoria will see fit to tell Weymouth. I only hope he doesn't call me out."

"Don't be absurd. You've done nothing to warrant a duel."

"Ah, but will he think so? Especially if his wife tells him that she wishes to leave him?"

Edward whistled. "Is that why she wanted to see you?"

Richard shrugged. "Let's forget it for now. I'm anxious to see your cousin before my reputation is so blackened that no one will receive me."

Edward turned the horses and set them to a brisk trot. "No need to worry about Lizzie. She's a loyal little beggar. As long as you're honest with her, she'll stand by you no matter what the tattle-boxes say."

It was fortunate for Richard that Edward could not see his face at that moment. His dismay was written clearly on his features. He'd not been completely honest—neither with Edward nor Elizabeth, and he'd have to do something about that soon. He supposed the wisest thing would be not to see Elizabeth Fairchild at all, and the thought of that depressed him. Still, he was being unfair to her. He was in no position, as yet, to court anyone. He decided he would allow himself this one afternoon in her company, and then stay away from her until his affairs were in order.

Edward brought his carriage to a neat stop in St. Charles Street, directly in front of the Davenport house. A boy was summoned to hold the horses, and the gentlemen hurried up the steps. It was already a quarter past the hour, and Mrs. Davenport was a stickler for punctuality.

The door opened at once, and Edward was forced to take a step backward as two young ladies emerged with their abigail.

"Why, Lord Edward, how delightful to see you," Cordelia Brookhurst simpered. "And you, too, Mr. Danvers."

Edward nodded curtly. They had wasted no time in rushing to spread their gossip, and his disdain clearly showed.

Carolyn turned to Richard and tapped her fan against his shoulder. "We were so disappointed you were unable to attend our rout, sir."

Richard bowed politely. "Unfortunately, Dr. Halymont would not allow me to leave my bed."

"But you're fully recovered now, aren't you, Mr. Danvers?" Cordelia said, with a sly look at Carolyn.

"Of course he is," her sister answered. "Didn't you observe how capably he was using both of his arms in the Park?" She tittered shrilly before sweeping past them.

CHAPTER SIX

WHEN THEY WERE SHOWN INTO the drawingroom a few minutes later, Miss Fairchild greeted her cousin warmly before turning to his friend.

"La, Mr. Danvers, we'd quite given you up for lost, since it's well past the hour."

"Give the gentleman a chance, Elizabeth. I'm certain he was not *willingly* detained," Mrs. Davenport chided her. "Come in, sir, and you, too, Edward. Be seated."

"I do apologize, Mrs. Davenport, Miss Fairchild. Is there anything I can do to make amends?"

Elizabeth busied herself with the teacups, and it was her great-aunt who, after a pause, answered. "Come sit beside me, Mr....er...Danvers. I wish to puzzle out your people."

Richard took his seat in the gilded armchair she indicated, and had to trust that Edward would plead his cause with Elizabeth.

"Now then, young man, my niece tells me you were born in Yorkshire. What part?"

"Just outside a small village, ma'am," Richard said evasively. "It's unlikely that you would have ever encountered my family. My father was not wealthy, and I doubt he moved in the same sort of circles as you."

"And *I* doubt that you would know anything to say to the matter. Not all my acquaintances are wealthy, or even members of the peerage. When you reach my age, you'll have learned that wealth is a poor measure of a man's worth.''

"I offer you my apologies again, Mrs. Davenport. That was presumptuous of me. But I only meant that my parents never entertained, and it was a rare occasion when anyone visited our estate.'' And that was odd, Richard thought, as it suddenly occurred to him that the seclusion in which his parents had lived was extremely unnatural.

Horatia Davenport didn't seem to consider it so. She was nodding her head in agreement. "My first husband was that way. Said he liked having me to himself. Reginald. Ah, now there was a real gentleman. Not like these namby-pamby creatures who flock after Lizzie.''

"He must have been a Corinthian to have won your approval, ma'am," Richard said, smiling.

"Indeed. You might not think it to look at me now, but I was a belle in my day. The toast of London. I could have married a duke had I been of a mind to.'' She glared at Richard as though he might doubt her word.

"You would have made a splendid duchess. In fact, there is something rather regal about you.''

"Don't be offering me Spanish coin just when I was beginning to like you, young man. Reginald never did, though he swept me off my feet. I told my papa I'd have him or no one.'' As she smiled at the recollection, her eyes misted and she peered closer at Richard. "You remind me a little of him.''

Richard breathed easier. There were no Reginalds in his family tree.

"Oh, not in looks, I'll admit. Reginald was much more dashing. No, as far as your looks go, it's someone else you put me in mind of. Perhaps one of my other suitors.''

"You must have had so many that I am certain it would be difficult to recall just one."

Her tiny dark eyes twinkled, and her chin quivered with laughter as she waved aside his nonsense. "Very pretty, sir. Now see if you can turn my niece up sweet. Lizzie, give Mr. Danvers a cake. I'm certain he is faint with hunger, and cannot think clearly."

"Certainly," Elizabeth replied coolly, and Richard watched as she gracefully sliced the cake and handed him a plate. Their hands brushed and he knew from the startled look in her eyes that she, too, felt the shock which passed between them.

Mrs. Davenport watched them with interest, and then motioned to Salford. "Come, Edward, I wish your opinion. Your mother tells me you've an interest in art. I just purchased a new painting by Constable which he calls *The Stour*. I should like to know how you think he compares to Gainsborough."

Edward, whose interest in art came as a surprise to him, obediently followed her from the room.

Elizabeth, embarrassed by her aunt's obvious ploy, spoke hurriedly. "Are you interested in art, also, Mr. Danvers? Would you care to see the gallery?"

"I don't think I would care to disoblige your great-aunt, Miss Fairchild."

"I scarce think you need worry, sir. Aunt Horatia seems to hold a good opinion of you."

"Which you do not share?"

"Are people from your part of the world always so direct? In England, gentlemen are less..."

"Forthright?" he supplied, laughing, and was absurdly pleased to see her smile. "I know that is a failing of mine, and yet your cousin assures me that you value honesty above all else."

"I do value honesty, sir, and abhor double-dealing or deceit of any sort." It was a gentle rebuke for keeping her waiting while he dallied with Lady Weymouth, and the look she wore was more hurt than angry.

"I can only ask you to believe that I am sincerely sorry to have been late today. There is not a person in the world whose good opinion I value more than your own, Miss Fairchild."

"If we are to deal honestly together, then I won't pretend to be unaware of how you spent your afternoon, sir, and that would seem to contradict your sentiment."

"Appearances can be misleading. I know the Brookhurst sisters saw me in the Park with Lady Weymouth, and unfortunately, just as their carriage passed, Lady Weymouth tripped. I caught her to prevent her from falling. I know it must have looked scandalous, but I swear it was an innocent gesture."

"It sounds most plausible, Mr. Danvers, and yet I can't help wondering how it came about that you were alone on the footpath with Lady Weymouth. Not that it is any concern of mine."

"The lady sent me a note asking that I meet her. She said the matter was urgent." He spread his hands in a helpless gesture. "I didn't feel I had any choice."

"Of course not. You are ever the knight-errant, and would naturally fly to a lady's rescue." Her voice was light, and her brown eyes teasing.

"Ah, now you are mocking me, but at least your eyes are smiling again. Miss Fairchild—"

"Please, I think you may use my name, sir."

"Thank you, Elizabeth. What I started to say was that it occurred to me while we were driving here that I should perhaps tell you something about my past." He hesitated, searching for the right words, but before he could speak, Mrs. Davenport returned with Edward close behind her.

"Well, Mr. Danvers, have you had sufficient time to make amends with my niece? No need to answer me. I can tell from just looking at Lizzie that she is no longer angry. And that is fortunate. Lizzie, your cousin has invited us to the theatre on Friday, and of course Mr. Danvers will be of the party."

Richard looked to Edward in surprise, but his friend merely shrugged, and then tried to appear nonchalant as Mrs. Davenport turned to address him.

"That's settled, then. Edward, you may call for us at eight. And mind you, be here promptly. I shall accept no more excuses for tardiness."

Richard, in a fairly bemused state, left with Edward. So much for his plan not to see Elizabeth again until his affairs were in order.

"I say, Richard, you don't object to the scheme, do you? I give you my word it was as much a surprise to me as it was to you. The great-aunt has it in her head that you'll do for Lizzie, and how do you gainsay her?"

"Her methods may lack subtlety, but they are certainly effective. I've no real objection," Richard assured him. "Only I had intended to concentrate my energies on getting Weycross Abbey back."

"I don't see any reason why you can't enjoy a little social life at the same time, and I'll help you. Now, what's to be done?"

"If it were only that simple, but thank you, Edward. You're a good friend. At present, there's nothing I can do, though perhaps I shall know more after I talk with Lord Demeral on Tuesday."

"Demeral? What's he got to do with your Abbey? Never tell me your father lost it to him!"

"No, the boot's on the other foot. Demeral lost his fortune to the same man who cheated my father. He mentioned it just in passing last night. That was the reason why I invited him to dine. I hope to find out more."

"I recall hearing something about that. I was up at Eton at the time, but even there one hears things, and I believe it was rather a scandal. My father would likely know, if anyone does. If you want, I could ask him."

"I think we should hear what Demeral has to say first. You could do one thing for me, however."

Edward eyed him reluctantly, not liking the look in Richard's eyes. He swallowed before declaring loyally, "You've only to ask it, of course."

"Steady on, dear friend, I promise you it's nothing drastic. I was only thinking that you could perhaps keep an eye on Victoria. She enacted me a pretty tragedy in the Park, and claims Weymouth abuses her."

"That prosy old windbag? I'd stake my life against it."

"That was my impression, too, but he could behave differently in private. The servants would know."

"If Lady Weymouth can't wind her husband round her little finger, she's not half the woman I thought her. But I shall find out, never fear. When I was a boy, I fancied myself a Bow Street Runner, and used to spy on my brother. Caught him out in a couple of ticklish situations, too. Don't imagine I've lost my touch."

"Edward, you will be discreet, won't you?"

"Trust me, Richard, and don't you worry. If Lady Weymouth is up to something, I'll ferret it out right enough."

Richard left him, but not without misgivings. He would've been further alarmed had he been privileged to see Lord Edward at dinner that evening. His friend watched Lady Weymouth so closely that Victoria thought he was trying to get up a flirtation. Her husband scowled at Edward, to little effect, while the duchess, fearing he was infatuated, began forming plans to send her favourite son out of Town.

Richard, blissfully unaware of his friend's antics, spent the evening quietly at home. After an excellent dinner, he retired to the library. With stationery and quill before him, he tried to concentrate on his plans and formulate a list. The first item was to see Lord Edward's solicitor, the same man that the duke used. If their solicitor put forth an offer to buy Weycross Abbey, he might produce better results than Richard's man had done. Surely, such a prestigious offer would force Pembroke out of the woodwork. Edward thought it an excellent idea, and Richard agreed.

What else? Richard found his mind wandering and brought his attention sharply back to the list. He gazed at the page in disbelief. He had mindlessly scrawled Elizabeth's name several times. Crumpling the paper, Richard cursed. The girl was proving a damnable distraction. If he was going to regain his lands, he needed to focus all his wits and energy to that end. Charming as Elizabeth was, he could not afford the distraction. He resolved not to see her again after the evening at the theatre. At least, not until his affairs were settled.

Feeling that he was behaving, in some manner, very nobly, he poured himself a brandy. *How odd,* Richard thought, *that I must force myself to think of Father. All those years in India, I could hardly think of anything else but getting to England and avenging him. Now that I'm finally here, it doesn't seem quite as important.*

He pulled open the bottom drawer of the pedestal desk and removed a small, black Chinoiserie box. Richard placed it carefully in the centre of the desk and slowly opened it. He stared at the stack of letters from his father for several minutes. Then, taking a sip of brandy, Richard untied the purple ribbon which bound them. He'd not read any of the letters for several years. Had not needed to, for the contents were burned into his memory. Each letter had brought, with its disastrous news, a bleak period of depression for Richard.

He removed the top letter from its envelope and studied the heavily creased page with its spidery handwriting. Even now, the letters had the power to disturb him. The blue eyes took on a hard look, and his mouth was set in grim lines.

His father's hatred for Pembroke spewed forth from the page, vilifying the man as the basest of creatures.

He means to destroy me, son, and the solicitors tell me he has bought up all my vowels. There is nothing left to sell. The bastard owns almost everything, and yet still encroaches like a vulture with its prey. I fear nothing will satisfy him but my death.

Richard returned the letter to its envelope with shaking hands. Carefully, he replaced the box in the desk drawer, and then drew stationery before him. He had no difficulty concentrating now, and no thoughts of Elizabeth intruded as he made his plans. After meeting with Demeral, he would ride north and inspect the Abbey for himself. He could assess the damage and estimate the cost of restoring the house. And he could talk to the people there. The country folks—perhaps even his old nurse. Richard added her name to his list.

During the following days, Richard continued to concentrate all his efforts on his plans. Locking himself in the library, he read and reread all his father's letters and ventured out only to visit the solicitor. On Friday morning, he set aside his plans with a clear conscience, and thought of the theatre and his evening with Elizabeth. Just thinking of her brought a smile to his lips—the first in several days.

Richard was still at the breakfast table when Philbin brought him a letter. His butler proffered it on a salver, his whole manner disapproving. "It was just delivered, sir, by an urchin. An extremely grubby, dirty, little boy."

"Thank you," Richard replied, his smile disappearing. He didn't have to open it to know that it was from Lady Weymouth. Through the dirty smudges that now covered it, the scent of violets assailed his nostrils. With a grimace of distaste, Richard withdrew the note.

My Dearest Richard

I beg you to help me. I fear Weymouth is losing his mind, and is crazed with jealousy. He threatens me daily, and has me watched day and night so that I fear for my life. I can only pray this note reaches you. I have a fitting tomorrow at Madame Dusante's in Bond Street. There is a back entrance that gives out onto the alley behind her shoppe. Please, *mon cher*, meet me there at two o'clock. Do not fail me, Richard, if ever you cared for your Victorie.

Richard read the note through twice before tossing it on the tray. Then retrieving it quickly, and folding it neatly, he placed it in his watch pocket. Was this more of Victoria's play-acting, or was she really in danger from Weymouth? Not for the first time, Richard wished Josiah were still alive. He would know how to deal with Victoria.

Philbin returned again, this time to announce Lord Edward. Salford took the seat opposite, and after declining all offers of refreshment, waited eagerly for Philbin to retire.

"Richard, I have so much to tell you, I scarce know where to begin. I have been following Lady Weymouth as you instructed—"

"As I instructed? Egad, Edward, I never told you—"

"Don't quibble, just listen. Your Lady Weymouth has been meeting someone secretly. I don't know who yet, but give me a few more days and I shall know everything. I have a talent for this sort of thing."

"Please don't refer to her as *my* Lady Weymouth. How do you know she's meeting someone?"

"I told you, I've been following her. Don't look like that. I promise you I've been utterly discreet, and I doubt the lady has any notion."

Richard could not suppress a grin. He withdrew Victoria's note and passed it across to Edward. The look of chagrin on his friend's face as he read her letter was enough to set Richard in whoops.

"Damn it all, Richard, stop laughing. I have been discreet. Perhaps Weymouth has someone else watching her, too... unless Dawes was careless."

"Dawes? You have your valet spying on her? Oh, Lord!"

"Well, I couldn't always get away myself. You needn't worry. Dawes is devoted to me, and completely loyal."

"I hope so. I shudder to think what the duchess would say should Lady Weymouth complain to her that her son and his valet are following her every movement."

Edward looked stricken for a moment, and then brightened. "She'd never complain to Mother. Not when she's been meeting someone clandestinely. Lady Weymouth complained of a headache last night and supposedly retired to her rooms. But we were ready for her. She left by the south drawing room terrace, and there was a hackney coach waiting for her. I couldn't see who was in it, but I'm certain it was a man."

"Did you follow the carriage?"

"How? We weren't expecting a carriage. But the next time I'll have my own curricle waiting. Then we shall see."

Richard nodded, reaching across for Victoria's note. "She says she thinks Weymouth is losing his mind. Have you learned anything from the servants?"

"Dawes is turning her dresser up sweet, though he says I should pay him extra, for she is the plainest woman, and haughty to boot. *She* is all on Victoria's side. She says Weymouth rants at her in private and makes all manner of accusations. And, on Wednesday morning, my lady had to cover a bruise on her cheek with a patch. The dresser thinks Weymouth struck her, but Victoria wouldn't say."

"Damn, I don't like the sound of that. There can be no excuse for striking a woman. Only a cowardly cad would do such a thing."

"Don't get in a taking, Richard. We don't know how she got the bruise."

"My apologies. You're right, of course. It's just that Josiah was always emphatic about that sort of thing. He drilled it into me when I was a boy that a gentleman never raises his hand to a lady. No matter what the provocation."

"No gentleman would, of course. Have you any idea who Victoria might be meeting?"

"None. She said I'm the only friend she has in England."

"Obviously, she knows at least one other. Well, Dawes will watch her this evening while we're at the theatre, although I don't think there's any chance of a rendezvous tonight. Mother has one of her political dinners planned, and Weymouth will insist his wife be present. The only opportunity she'll have will be this afternoon. I'm going back now to relieve Dawes. I'll fetch you later this evening."

Richard wondered idly what the duchess would think of her son's aptitude for spying. Perhaps the duke could use Edward's natural talents in his political efforts on behalf of England. Richard grinned at the thought. Edward's efforts would probably turn out to be as much a farce as the comedy they would see this evening. Thinking of the evening brought Elizabeth to mind, and he hurried off to consult with Roscoe on his evening attire.

ROSCOE DID HIS MASTER proud, and such was his appearance that Edward was moved to whistle in approval as Richard came down the stairs that evening. He wore a dark blue satin tailcoat, with a black velvet collar over tightly fitting white pantaloons. His stock was of only medium height, but Roscoe had used a tie of black velvet and an ornamental diamond stick pin to set it off. With his black beaver hat and cane, Richard was looking extremely handsome.

Great-Aunt Horatia agreed, but lest he become puffed up in his own conceit, she commented that in her day, gentlemen powdered their hair, or else donned a wig for an evening affair. Her own wig was elaborately curled and piled high on her head. Diamonds twinkled here and there as she nodded, and Richard told her he was honoured to be seen in the company of such a grande dame.

She did indeed look regal with her diamonds and a deep purple silk dress, but it was Elizabeth who brought the look of delight to his eyes. She wore a white silk gown, covered with several layers of blue gauze. It was low cut, and a large blue sapphire nestled just above her breasts, leaving Richard momentarily speechless. Her large brown eyes looked up at him provocatively as she waited for his comment.

"Well, sir, am I to take it that you can find nothing to say of a complimentary nature?"

"Nothing that has not been said a thousand times to a thousand women, none of whom could compare with your beauty."

"Dash it all, Richard," Edward complained, "if you keep paying such extravagant compliments to the ladies, you'll leave me with nothing to say, and make me look no-how."

"Extravagant?" Elizabeth turned to her cousin, "Do you disagree with Richard, then? And it was such a pretty compliment."

"And I suppose you think I look less than a grande dame?" Horatia added. "You would do well, Edward, to study Mr. Danvers's style."

Edward reddened and made haste to apologize, but the ladies only laughed at him. The drive to the theatre passed quickly as the nonsense continued, and the four arrived in high good humour.

Mrs. Davenport maintained a private loge, and as hostess, directed the seating. Richard sat in front, with Elizabeth between him and Edward. The great-aunt took her place beside Edward, and proceeded to use her quizzing glass to stare at the notables arriving. She took great pleasure in minutely examining their attire and pointing out any faults to Edward.

Elizabeth was left to entertain Richard, and she could not help but be aware of all the looks cast in their direction.

"Lord, sir, I fear we will be tomorrow's on-dit, particularly since you've been absent from any affairs this week."

"You flatter me. I doubt that any but such kind friends as you and your cousin noticed my absence."

"Indeed, Richard, you underestimate yourself. A presentable young man with a vast fortune, in London to seek a wife, will always be the cynosure of the ton's attention. Only look at Lady Bromwich staring at us."

Richard reluctantly withdrew his attention from the delicate lines of her face and glanced in the direction she pointed with her fan. An elderly dowager was certainly watching them closely. His eyes roved past her and around the vast hall, and he was tempted to wave at a number of young ladies who stared at him from behind their fans. His gaze passed over one young raven-haired beauty and abruptly returned. It was not the young lady, however, who drew his attention, but the older woman sitting beside her.

Lady Blanche Sewell was an elegant matron, and one of the few who did not try to hide her age. Her greying hair was swirled up in an intricate, but soft, coiffure, which became the small oval face. She had a gentle look about her. Richard thought her one of the most beautiful women he had ever seen. He had thought so when he was only ten, and Lady Blanche had visited his mother.

"You are looking at the new toast of the ton. That is Lady Anne Sewell, and she is quite as pleasant as she is pretty," Elizabeth told him as she watched him staring at the box opposite.

"Very fetching," Richard agreed, bringing his gaze back to Elizabeth, "if one has a preference for brunettes."

Loud clapping and a few boisterous calls heralded the beginning of the farce. Richard turned his eyes to the stage without seeing any of the comedy, his mind still on Lady Sewell. Visions from his boyhood danced before his eyes. His mother had told him that she and Lady Sewell had attended school together, and had been fast friends. It was hard for a ten-year-old to imagine two ancient ladies as ever being schoolgirls, and Lady Sewell had laughed, though not unkindly, at his amazement. Richard recalled his father had been away on some sort of visit that month. It was one of his more pleasant memories. He remembered his mother laughing a great deal, and there had been picnics and long rambling walks across the fields.

He glanced again to the opposite box, though he could see nothing but darkness above the bright light of the stage. It was doubtful that Lady Sewell would recognize him, but his name would give her pause. Danvers was his mother's maiden name, and she would surely recall Laura Danvers's tow-headed son, Richard.

The applause startled him, and Richard realized belatedly that the first act was over. He joined in the applause, before politely enquiring if Elizabeth was enjoying the play.

"It's truly wonderful," she replied, with no more idea than he what had occurred on the stage. His presence beside her had proven too much of a distraction, and her stolen glances at his profile had convinced her that his thoughts were elsewhere.

"I'm glad you're enjoying it," Richard replied. "Do you care for refreshment, or perhaps a stroll?"

"Nothing, thank you. I'm quite content to simply sit here."

There was a gentle rap on the door, and one of the attendants appeared, "Mr. Richard Danvers?"

Richard nodded, and the young man presented him with a note. "I'm to wait for an answer, sir, if that's agreeable?"

He was too surprised to do more than nod, and Elizabeth smiled at him. "Go ahead and read it, Richard. No doubt it is from one of your admirers here, wishing for an assignation."

His head bent and he read the few lines rapidly. Elizabeth thought he paled slightly, but it was difficult to tell in the dim light.

"Tell Lady Sewell that I thank her, and I shall be delighted to call on her tomorrow."

CHAPTER SEVEN

RICHARD AWOKE with an aching head, which Roscoe did not hesitate to ascribe to the amount of brandy his master had consumed the evening before. He was even unfeeling enough to yank open the heavy curtains, flooding the room with sunlight.

Richard made a sound halfway between a growl and a groan, but Roscoe ignored him and continued to deliver a homily on the wages of sin, and of excess indulgence in particular.

"The old man was probably turning in his grave last night, knowing his heir came home as drunk as a wheelbarrow. You was so badly dipped, me and Kirby had to cart you up the stairs. Fine goings-on, it is."

Richard's hand reached out and encountered a heavy glass tumbler on the bedside table. "One more word—" he threatened, raising the glass. "Bring up coffee at once, and spare me any more of your lectures, or I swear you'll find yourself mucking out the stables."

Roscoe grinned to himself as he stepped into the hall and motioned for the footman to bring in the coffee tray. He'd been worried when his young lord had come home from the theatre so melancholy last evening. This was more like it.

He busied himself about the room, giving Richard time to drink his coffee, and waited for instructions, which were not long in coming. Richard demanded the time, and on learning it was close to noon, ordered Town dress. He had not forgotten that Victoria wanted to meet him at two, and he had the interview with Lady Sewell at four. And for all his deliberations the night before, he still had not decided what to tell Blanche Sewell. His situation was awkward in the extreme.

He decided against telling Roscoe of either of his engagements. The first would only bring forth a torrent of remonstrations, and the second, dire predictions of disaster. Roscoe would assume that he was meeting Lord Edward and that, at least, had his valet's approval.

Nor could he allow Kirby to drive him. That was the worst of having devoted servants. One of these days, he vowed silently, he would engage a tiger to ride behind him. One who would not give a tinker's damn if his master made strange assignations. Regrettably, there was not enough time to engage such a person, and he decided to leave on foot, and then hire a hackney.

He barely managed to escape the house in time, for both Kirby and Roscoe had been loud in their protests, and neither had hesitated to remind him of what had occurred the last time he left the house alone. His head still ached abominably, and he had hoped to leave with ample time to stop and order flowers delivered to Elizabeth. He felt he owed her an apology of sorts.

After he had received Lady Sewell's note, the rest of the evening had passed in a blur for Richard. He had tried to act natural, but he had been preoccupied, and Elizabeth, too, had been strangely silent. Only Mrs. Davenport had been voluble, demanding to know how he came to be acquainted with Lady Sewell. He knew his evasive answers had not satisfied her and she would no doubt pursue their conversation at the first opportunity.

The carriage stopped at the corner Richard indicated, and bidding the driver wait, he got out feeling extremely self-conscious. He glanced in at Madame Dusante's as he passed, but it was full of feminine apparel, as well as a number of young ladies, and he looked hurriedly away. He rounded the corner into the alley, and then wondered what he should do. If he simply loitered near the door, he was bound to attract attention. The alley was not long, less than a quarter mile, he judged. He could stroll down the alley, and then return. His watch showed just a few minutes past the hour. Surely it would not take Victoria long to pass through the salon and out the rear entrance.

Richard tried to assume a casual air as he sauntered down the alley. Rubbish littered both sides of the narrow dirt lane, and it was not at all the sort of destination a gentleman would willingly choose for a stroll. He felt conspicuous, and somewhat foolish, as he reached the end of the alley, turned and retraced his steps.

He was only a few feet away when the door to Madame Dusante's opened, and Victoria stepped out. Although the day was warm, she was heavily veiled, and Richard thought it must be obvious to anyone watching that a clandestine meeting was taking place. Victoria extended her hands.

"Ah, Richard, my dearest Richard. I knew in my heart that you would not fail me."

"I was of course concerned when I received your note, Lady Weymouth. Any *friend* would be. Are you certain there is need for us to meet this way?"

Without a word, Victoria freed her hands and lifted the veil from her cheek. Richard blanched. A livid, purple bruise covered most of her right cheek. She quickly dropped the veil again, placing a hand gently on his arm.

Her voice was no more than a husky whisper. "You see why I had to see you, *mon cher.*"

"Who did this to you, Victoria?"

"Can you not guess, Richard? I have told you how I am abused. But this . . . this is nothing. I am accustomed to William's rages, and small bruises on my body. It is the price I pay for being Lady Weymouth."

They could not conduct this conversation standing in the alley. Richard saw nothing for it but to put her in his carriage. Victoria went with him willingly, and Richard tersely directed the driver to take them as far as the Park and then return.

He sat silently beside her for a few minutes, endeavouring to control his rage. That a man, any man, should so abuse a woman sickened him.

"Why, Victoria? Why does Weymouth abuse you? I should have sworn that he doted on you."

"Oh, he does, *mon cher.* That is the problem. If I so much as smile at another gentleman, he flies into a violent, jealous rage. He is, always, most apologetic afterward. And always, he swears he will never hit me again." She paused, fingering a large, emerald brooch which secured her pelisse. "This was a gift after one incident." A heavy gold bracelet encircled her wrist, and she lifted it. "This, after another. I have a box full of jewels—all testimonials to William's jealousy."

"How could you stay with such a man? Surely, your uncle—"

"No! A thousand times no. My uncle would not lift a finger to help me. He is one of those who consider a wife to be her husband's chattel."

"But if you told him—"

"I have, Richard. Ah, my friend, you are such an innocent. Not all men are like you, dear one. Uncle Clarence laughed when I told him how William abused me. He said I should not provoke him, and that Weymouth was what I needed to...to keep me in line. I *cannot*, I will not go to him."

She seemed on the verge of tears, and Richard lapsed into silence, trying desperately to think of what he could do to help.

Victoria's voice, muffled by the heavy veil, lilted softly in his ear. "Richard, I remember, always, the enchanted times with you. Do you recall how it was? You and I, darling, we could be happy together. With you, I would go anywhere. We could even go back to India."

"Victoria, you cannot know what you are saying."

"I do, Richard. I do. I have thought much of it. Society would shun us, but that would not matter if we were together. I could make you happy, Richard. Enough to forget the rest of the world. We could make each other happy."

The scent of violets was overpowering as she leaned close against him, and Richard longed to raise the shade, but dared not.

"Victoria, things have changed. I...I don't...I cannot leave England. There are matters here which I must attend to. But I will help you. I'll find a place where you can stay in safety, and I'll engage a solicitor for you. He'll help you file for a bill of divorcement."

There was silence as she calculated rapidly. This was not the offer she wanted, but perhaps it would do for a start. It could work to her advantage.

"Thank you, Richard. I knew I could depend on you. I had hoped—but that was foolish of me. I shall be grateful, *mon cher,* for whatever you can do."

Expecting tears, or other feminine wiles, Richard was agreeably surprised at her soft voice. He swore he would begin searching for a house at once.

"I shall send you word through Lord Edward as soon as I've located a suitable place."

"Lord Edward? Oh, please Richard, don't. I would rather no one else knew. I could not bear to face him otherwise." She appeared to consider the matter, and then suggested, "I will call at Madame Dusante's every day. Leave word there for me. I know I can trust Madame."

Although he loathed the thought of entering that establishment, Richard agreed. The carriage halted, and he cautiously raised the shade. They were back at Bond Street. He stepped out first, and after a guarded look round, handed Victoria down.

She pressed his hand to her breast. "I will never be able to thank you enough, dearest Richard."

"We will not speak of gratitude, Victoria. Now hurry, before you are seen." He watched her enter the shop, and then to satisfy his curiosity, strolled out front. He stood a little concealed behind a tree and watched. Victoria came out and entered the carriage waiting for her. Findley was driving, and Richard watched him tool the vehicle down Bond Street. A minute later, a second carriage followed. Could it have been Edward? Would he have bothered following Victoria today? Edward had read Victoria's note and knew he was meeting her. Richard felt a trace of uneasiness. He had not recognized the driver, and if he was not one of Edward's minions, then it seemed likely Weymouth was indeed having his wife followed.

His own driver interrupted his thoughts with a demand to know if he was wanted any longer. Richard nodded and gave the man directions to Lady Sewell's. He wished he had time to change first. The encounter with Victoria had been draining. The back of his shirt was damp, and his collar was certainly wilting. He doubted the interview with Lady Sewell would be any less emotional.

Richard was shown to a pretty salon that gave out onto a small, colourful garden. The room was painted a golden yellow with white trim, and with the French doors standing wide, it had the charming effect of a fresh, spring day. It looked altogether peaceful, and his first thought was how well it suited Lady Sewell.

She was seated on a delicate Chippendale sofa near the doors. Richard paused inside the room, waiting for her to speak.

Blanche Sewell rose and stretched out her hands in a warm welcome. "Come in, Richard, and let me have a look at you. It's been too many years since I have had that pleasure."

He smiled and crossed to her. The clear grey eyes looked him over, and she seemed pleased with what she saw.

"There was a time when I had to bend to kiss your cheek. Now it is you who will have to stoop."

Richard did so gladly, strangely touched by her gentleness, and seated himself next to her.

"If Anne could only see you, she would be most pleased."

"You and my mother were very close, I remember."

She nodded. "We were like sisters. I even named my daughter for her."

"Lady Anne. Yes, I saw her with you last night. Miss Fairchild pointed her out, and told me she is as pleasant as she is pretty."

"Thank you," she said, handing him his cup of tea.

The silence stretched between them, and Richard suddenly felt uncomfortable. "I suppose you are wondering why I'm not using my title?"

"When I heard that young Mr. Richard Danvers had arrived in Town from India, I suspected it was too much of a coincidence for it to be anyone but you, but I was not certain until I saw you at the theatre. I suppose you learned your father—"

"Was cheated out of our lands and hounded to death? Yes, Lady Sewell, and I intend to avenge his honour and reclaim the Estate. Once I settle the score with Lord Pembroke, I'll take my rightful place."

"With Pembroke? Richard, I don't quite understand."

"It was Rowland Pembroke who drove my father to his death and stole his lands. I swore when Father died that I'd make the man pay for his infamy, but thus far, Lord Pembroke has been strangely elusive."

"Your father actually wrote you about Lord Pembroke?"

"Every letter I received from him was full of hatred for the man. In his very last letter to me, Father said he was like a vulture, and would be satisfied only by his own death."

"I see. And did St. Symington write you about Anne, as well?"

"No. I fear he was too deeply grieved by her death. There was only a line or two telling me she'd died. Were you with her at the end? Did you see her, Lady Sewell?"

Blanche did not answer him at once, her kind eyes reflecting the sorrow she was feeling. She chose her words carefully, not wishing to hurt him. "The last time I visited Anne, her only thoughts were of you. I know she was deeply troubled by the knowledge that she might never see you again.''

''I was hoping to hear she forgave me for my stupidity. Did she tell you that I would not answer her letters?''

Blanche nodded sadly, and the compassion Richard saw in her eyes encouraged him to speak of his mother as he had not done in years.

''When I was seven or eight, I used to follow her about like a puppy. I did whatever I could to help her. To me, she was the most wonderful person in the world. Then things seemed to change. There were times when I was not allowed near her rooms, and I wouldn't see her for several days.''

''Richard, there were reasons for what must have seemed like strange behaviour to you,'' she said, and laid a hand on his arm. Her eyes met his directly. ''Never doubt that Anne loved you.''

''I tried to believe that, but she did send me away. About as far as she could possibly send me. They argued about it, my parents. Father didn't want me to go, but she was insistent. I think for a time, I hated her. I wouldn't even read her letters at first, although I read them all later. Read them until they fell apart. By then she had stopped writing. Father seldom mentioned her in his letters, not until she died. And then it was too late to tell her how I felt.''

''She knew, Richard. Please believe that. She knew how you felt, and how it must've looked to you. But Anne did what she thought was best for you. There were problems—''

''I know. She told me how heavily we were in debt, and how Josiah could help me. I don't blame her now, Lady

Sewell. Once I've brought Pembroke to book, I shall build a monument to her."

"Richard, you keep referring to Lord Pembroke. What is it you think he did? Anne always spoke very kindly of him."

"My mother always spoke well of everyone. But my father wrote me how Pembroke cheated him. Whenever Father had an unfortunate loss at the gaming tables, Pembroke was always there to buy up his vowels. And he'd never allow Father to redeem them. He wanted the Abbey. And in the end, he succeeded. My solicitors tell me he owns everything but the house itself, and the few acres surrounding it."

"Richard, I pray that I'm a good Christian, and I know one should not speak ill of the dead, but I must tell you that your father was not the man you think him. The troubles he suffered, he brought upon himself through his drink and his gaming. I know Lord Pembroke. He only did what he could to help, and he was a true friend to Anne."

Richard stood, his back stiffening. "Forgive me, Lady Sewell, but you were always quick to criticize my father. Of course he drank and gambled. So do most of the peers. But at the end, he was ill and alone. Pembroke took advantage of him, and drove him to suicide. Not even you can find an excuse for that. And it's not as though Father was the only one. Lord Demeral tells me Pembroke cheated him of his fortune, too."

"Demeral? I don't believe I know the name."

"It hardly matters, and I beg you won't concern yourself. Trust that I know what I'm doing."

"I wish I could, Richard, but I fear you are making a grievous mistake. Can you not just put the past to rest? I know that is what your mother would wish."

"I believe you mean well, Lady Sewell, but this is a matter of honour. Only another gentleman would understand my position."

"Then I shall only ask that you do one thing to oblige me." She rose in agitation and hurried to the small secretary beneath the window. As she pulled out a quill and hurriedly wrote, she asked, "Do you recall Mrs. Chiltern?"

"My old nurse! Of course. In fact, I hope to visit her when I go North. Do you remember how I used to call her Chilly?"

Lady Sewell nodded in distraction. "I am writing out her direction for you. She is not in York any longer, but just outside of London in a small town called Runnymede. Go to her, Richard, and ask her to tell you of your mother."

"I should be delighted to see her again, of course, but I don't see—"

"I know," she said, handing him the slip of paper. "But indulge me in this. It is all I ask of you, and I ask it for the sake of Anne."

She had tears in her eyes, obviously overset, and Richard agreed without further argument. She had been kind to him as a boy, and it was, after all, a small thing she asked.

"Thank you, and I beg you will excuse me now. I must rest, but I should like you to call again, after you have seen Mrs. Chiltern. I shall send her a note to expect you."

He left her in the salon, somehow looking small and forlorn. He felt an absurd sense of guilt, and tried to ease it by telling himself that women didn't understand these matters. His thoughts drifted to his mother, and therein lay his true guilt.

He had loved her so much, and when she sent him away, he had reacted spitefully, refusing to have anything to do with her. But he had never stopped loving her, and had intended one day to make amends. The notion that she might die had simply never occurred to him. And then it was too late.

Richard had been devastated, but no less so than Josiah. His father had written to the old man, as well, and Josiah had locked himself in his rooms for several days. He had drunk himself senseless, according to the servants. When he had at last come out and made an effort to comfort his adopted son, he found that Richard had dealt with his grief by denying it. Richard stubbornly refused to talk about his mother, and her name had not passed between them again until Josiah was dying.

Feeling unaccountably depressed, Richard looked about him, seeking a diversion. He had been walking aimlessly, and now he found himself in front of Mrs. Davenport's town house. He knew he should call on his solicitor and do something about a house for Victoria, but at present, he wanted more than anything else to see Elizabeth. And, after all, he reasoned, he did owe her an apology.

The butler informed him that Mrs. Davenport was resting, and Lady Fairchild was not at home. Miss Fairchild, however, was in the garden. The butler left him at the terrace door, and Richard saw Elizabeth among the roses. He stood watching her for several minutes, until her pet spaniel caught his scent and turned, barking noisily at the intruder.

"Quiet, Watts. Sit," Elizabeth ordered, but the spaniel only braced himself, put his ears back and barked all the more furiously as Richard advanced.

"Now I know I'm in disgrace," Richard told her, smiling. "You've set your dog upon me."

"I'm sorry, Richard. He gets these notions and thinks he's protecting me. Stay here, and I'll take him in."

Richard looked at the ball of fur trying to take a bite out of his boot. *"Sit!"* he commanded sharply, and the spaniel, hearing the voice of authority, immediately behaved. Richard knelt to his level. "Now, sir, what's the meaning of this?" he asked, holding the dog's head beneath the chin.

Ears cocked, tail wagging, the spaniel conveyed his apologies, and then further abased himself by wiggling forward on his stomach until he could lick Richard's hand.

Elizabeth laughed. "So much for my protector. Watts, you're a disgrace to your name."

"A strange name for the little fellow," Richard said, standing and dusting off his hands.

"He was named for Isaac Watts. 'Let dogs delight to bark and bite, For God hath made them so.' It seemed appropriate when he was a pup, for that was all he did do. But I thought I'd taught him better manners."

"Don't reproach him. It's my bad manners which are at fault. I entered his territory without leave."

"Nevertheless, you have his full approval now. Shall we go in, or would you prefer to sit out here for a few minutes?"

"Out here. The fresh air helps to blow the cobwebs from my mind."

She led him to a bench conveniently situated, and gestured for him to be seated. Watts waited patiently, and then positioned himself at Richard's feet, one paw laid possessively across his boot.

"Elizabeth, I feel I owe you an apology. Lady Sewell distracted me so much last night that I don't believe I put together two coherent sentences the entire evening. You must have thought me an abominable companion."

"No, only preoccupied," she answered, incurably honest. "It's not the first time I've seen a gentleman bedazzled by Lady Anne."

"Lady Anne? You thought—oh, Lord, I do owe you an apology. It wasn't Lady Anne, but her mother who claimed my attention. You see, she knew me when I was a boy. I hadn't seen her since I was ten, and coming across her suddenly like that was a little like seeing a ghost."

She studied him, and Richard noted how the sunlight filled her brown eyes with hazel lights.

"No apologies or explanations are necessary, Richard, though I should like to understand what it is that causes you such sorrow. There are times when your eyes take on a look of such...such sadness," she finished lamely. And didn't add that it was those times when she longed to brush the hair back from his brow and hold him close until the hurt had passed.

"You are the most remarkable girl," he told her. And neither noticed that somehow her hand was in his. The garden was still and peaceful, and for a moment only the drone of bees could be heard. Richard began quietly to tell her his story. He left nothing out, save his title, and the name of the man responsible for his father's death.

Elizabeth's maternal instincts were aroused. While she had admired Richard for his bravery, handsome bearing and easy address, her heart had not been completely engaged. Not as it was by this glimpse of an endearing little boy who had been cruelly hurt by his parents.

"You do understand, Elizabeth? My first priority must be to regain the estate and set my affairs in order. It's a vow I made long ago, and until I've done that and taken my rightful place, I can't approach your mother."

"Mother? But she—"

"Oh, Lord! I'm going about this all wrong. I hadn't meant to say anything yet. In fact, I hadn't meant to see you again—not until I could do so properly. Will you forget what I just said?"

Her laughter rang out, startling a blue jay. "Oh, Richard, you absurd, foolish, wonderful man. You half-propose to me, and then ask me to forget it. Do you fear you'll change your mind?"

Her happiness was contagious, and he reached up to caress a delicate cheek. "No fear of that. I think it was destined long ago. Only look how my heart led me here when I'd no intention of seeing you."

"Then trust your heart," she said softly. Their heads were close together, and it was the most natural thing in the world for Richard to draw her into a gentle embrace.

"Elizabeth!" The strident, demanding voice shattered the peace of the garden. Lady Fairchild stood before them, her breast heaving with her rage. "Go into the house at once. I will deal with *you* later."

"But, Mama, it is not what—"

"At once, Elizabeth."

She left slowly, with a last beseeching look at Richard. He squared his shoulders, preparing to explain the situation fully to Lady Fairchild, but was given no chance.

"You will leave this house at once, Mr. Danvers, or I shall call someone to evict you. I never want to see you near my daughter again."

"Lady Fairchild, I know it was improper of me to be here with Elizabeth, but if you will only allow me to explain—"

"Do not use her name. She is not for the likes of *you*." Not waiting to hear more, she turned on her heel and followed Elizabeth in, loudly slamming the door.

The noise had disturbed Horatia, and she peered from her upstairs window. She couldn't hear what Amelia was saying, but the intent was clear, and she half smiled. Amelia's wishes didn't concern her in the least. She would wed the chit where she chose, and at present young Mr. Danvers seemed an ideal choice. Then her breath caught. Why hadn't she seen it before? He was the image of James St. Symington. No wonder he had looked familiar. If it had not been for Reginald, she might have married St. Symington.

Richard must be related. His grandson, perhaps? She recalled the old scandal, and that the boy had been packed off. To India, of course. Why wasn't he using his name? Lord, bad blood there. This wouldn't do at all.

CHAPTER EIGHT

AT AN EARLY HOUR on Monday morning, Richard was seated in the private office of Mr. Julius H. Bailey, Sr., eldest member of the firm of Bailey & Downs, Solicitors. That he was not relegated to a junior member of the firm was an indication of the regard in which he was held. Richard may have been regrettably young, at least in the eyes of the elderly Mr. Bailey, but he was indisputably the wealthiest of all the firm's clients.

"Of course, my lord, of course," Bailey was saying. "We shall do our utmost to assist you, although I'm certain you will appreciate that these matters take time."

"I don't wish to be unreasonable, sir, but I no longer have the luxury of a great deal of time. There are pressing reasons why I must settle my affairs as rapidly as possible. If you feel procuring the Abbey lands are beyond your means, then I beg you to say so. My friend, Lord Edward Salford, has recommended his father's solicitors, Manchester & Cleeve."

"I assure you, Lord St. Symington, that there is not another firm who could act more promptly than Bailey & Downs, or one which has more skill in the delicate negotiations required in the acquisition of land, such as that involved with Weycross Abbey."

"Lord Edward seems to think that the duke's solicitor might be more successful in approaching Pembroke."

"Extremely unlikely, my lord. You are aware that Lord Pembroke refuses to see anyone other than his family and a few close friends, and that is what has prevented our negotiating with him. However, one of my junior members has an acquaintance with a young lady who is niece to Lord Pembroke. She invited him to accompany her on a visit to her uncle this past weekend. He should be there, even as we speak."

"Excellent. I felt certain I could rely on you. I shall be leaving for Yorkshire myself on Friday. I should like your report before I leave."

"*Friday*. Really, Lord St. Symington, I—"

"Friday. I also want you to find a suitable house for lease. It must be furnished, fully staffed and situated in a genteel, though quiet neighbourhood for a young lady and her companion. I shall need the lease by Thursday."

Mr. Bailey found himself bereft of words, and Richard added generously, "Engage additional staff, if that will help."

"Thank you, my lord, but my staff is adequate. The problem is that there may not *be* a suitable house available on such short notice. The Season has started."

"I have the utmost confidence in you, Mr. Bailey. You will have to know in any event, so I don't scruple to tell you that the house will be for Lady Weymouth. She and her husband are currently visiting the Duke of Cardiff. Lady Weymouth will also need your assistance in filing a bill of divorcement."

"I see," Bailey said, placing his fingertips together and pursing his mouth.

"I doubt it," Richard answered with a wry grin. "Do your best, however, and of course I'll foot all the bills."

He left the solicitor's office buzzing with speculation and dropped by White's in the hope of seeing Lord Edward. The doorman informed him that his friend had not been in the club for several days, and Richard reluctantly left a message for him, should he appear. Nor was Edward to be found at Watier's, his boxing club, Tattersall's, or any of his other haunts. Richard knew he would likely be more successful calling at the duke's residence, but he feared a chance meeting with Victoria, and that he wanted to avoid at all costs.

He left messages everywhere he could think it possible that Edward might visit, and then returned home to an excellent dinner. Richard consumed it without knowing or caring what he ate, his mind actively making plans. Philbin brought the brandy decanter out, but Richard waved it away.

"Bring me coffee in the library, please, Philbin. And tell Roscoe I wish to speak with him."

Philbin paused, and then coughed. "I beg your pardon, sir, but as I am head of your household, there is a matter which I feel I would be derelict in my duty did I not bring it to your attention."

"Yes?"

"It's your valet and groom, sir. I am aware that they came with you from India, and that they have been in your employ for a good many years, and while I make allowances for cultural differences, I cannot credit that you would engage staff who feel at liberty to wander in and out of the house at will. It is not something I can condone, not without your express approval, sir."

"Do you think, Philbin, that you could endeavour to be a trifle clearer? You are referring to Roscoe and Kirby?"

"Yes, sir. To be blunt, Mr. Danvers, they disappear for long stretches of time, and no one knows where they are. To any questions regarding their absence, they turn a deaf ear. Of course they are not under my direct supervision and I cannot ask for an accounting of their time, but I must say, with all respect, sir, that they are behaving in a dubious manner, to say the least.''

''I'll look into it, Philbin. Thank you.''

Richard moved into the library, and while he waited for his valet, he considered his butler's words. He should have realized something was afoot, for neither Roscoe nor Kirby had been plaguing him, which in itself was suspicious.

''You sent for me, sir?'' The wiry valet came in, much upon his dignity, for Richard had not been confiding in him of late.

''Sit down, Roscoe, we have much to discuss.''

''I'll stand, sir, if you don't mind.''

''As you please. Where is Kirby, by the way?''

''Kirby?''

The guilty start was all the proof Richard needed. ''Yes, Kirby. You remember him, surely?''

''I was jest surprised you asked. I don't normally keep track of your groom, sir. What would you be wantin' with Kirby?''

''I merely desired to know where he was. I understand he's been absent a great deal of late.''

''Oh, that. You know how is it, sir. I believe he's been stepping out with a housemaid a few doors down, and seeing as how you ain't been wanting him to drive you of late, he didn't think you'd object none.''

''I see. Well, I'll speak with him later. I wanted you to know that I plan to drive to York on Friday morning, and I shall take both you and Kirby with me. I expect we shall be gone for at least a week or two.''

"Yes, sir! That's what I've been telling Kirby all along. We should be up there at that Abbey of yours, and see what's what."

"Thank you, Roscoe. I'm glad my plans meet with your approval. I trust you will also approve my pending marriage. I can't reveal the lady's name as yet, because there are some problems that must be resolved before our engagement can be made official. However, I've spoken with her, and I've every expectation of wedding before the year is out."

"I'm sure I wish you happy, sir," Roscoe said, sounding far from it. Without thinking, he sat in the chair before the desk, shoulders hunched forward.

"Thank you. I trust you'll spare me any of your gloomy prophecies. Although I must admit that one of your dire predictions has come true. I was recognized at the theatre Friday evening by Lady Sewell."

Roscoe's head came up. "And didn't I tell you someone would be bound to know you? I knew we'd wind up in the basket before all was said and done."

"We're not in the basket yet. I visited the lady on Saturday, and she quite understands my desire to remain anonymous. She was a childhood friend of my mother's—one of the few visitors we had at the Abbey."

"And a lady like that is gonna be a party to your play-acting?"

"I'm hardly committing a crime. Lady Sewell understands well enough, and was, for the most part, sympathetic. Her only stipulation was that I should visit my old nurse. A lady you would, no doubt, admire greatly. She was in the habit of scolding me quite as much as you."

"I never—"

"The woman's name is Hannah Chiltern, and she resides in a place called Runnymede. You and Kirby, between you, should be able to find out where it is, and estimate how long it will take to drive there. I must see her either Wednesday or Thursday.''

"Yes, sir."

"I believe that's all," Richard said, glancing down at the papers on his desk. "Oh, there is one more thing. Mr. Bailey, or someone from his office may call. I've commissioned him to lease a house. Let me know at once if he calls while I'm out."

"Another house, sir?"

"Didn't I mention that? Lady Weymouth is leaving her husband, and she appealed to me for help. She hasn't many friends in London, you know. In light of our friendship, I am arranging a place for her to stay." He stared at Roscoe, daring him to say a word.

Roscoe knew his Master well enough to know when to hold his peace. He merely nodded and quit the room with slow, weary steps.

Richard smiled at the closed door. That should give Roscoe and Kirby something to think about. Let them both believe that he intended to wed Victoria. He was willing to wager his last pound that he knew what they had been up to. And if he was right, they would soon learn a much-needed lesson.

He picked up the stack of paper on his desk. If he didn't sell the company outright, then he would have to hire a secretary to help him deal with all the correspondence. Richard methodically sorted through the letters, calculating figures and carefully checking each item before neatly writing out his decision. Decisions which would not reach Calcutta for almost nine months. A delay which would cost him heavily. He worked steadily for two hours, and was glad of the interruption when Philbin knocked gently on the door.

"Excuse me, Mr. Danvers. Lord Edward is here, and wishes a word with you."

"Show him in, Philbin, and I think you may also serve the brandy now."

Edward entered, looking very smart in tailored evening dress, and Richard waved him to a chair. "You're just in time, Edward. I've sent Philbin for the brandy. Have you an engagement, or can you stay and have a glass?"

"I *had* an engagement. I was at Lady Dunhill's musicale, but when I heard what happened, I rushed over here."

"I was wishing for a chance to speak with you privately. In fact, I left messages for you all over Town." As the butler entered, he added, "Let me know what you think of this brandy. I'm told it was smuggled in from the coast at great peril."

Both gentlemen sampled the brandy, waiting for Philbin to withdraw. As soon as the door shut behind him, Edward demanded, "Richard, what the devil have you been doing? I just left Lizzie, and she told me she's being sent to Harrogate in disgrace. Did you know?"

"No, but I'm not altogether surprised. Did she tell you why?"

"We only had a moment together before Aunt Amelia whisked her away. As though I might contaminate her. Lizzie said her mother had learned of her attachment to you, and was totally opposed to the match. And then Aunt Amelia told me that I should choose my friends more carefully, and that if I must consort with commoners I could at least find one with the manners of a gentleman. *What* did you do to set her off? And what is this about a match? I knew you liked Lizzie—a man would have to be blind not to know, the way you look at her, but I didn't think you'd made a declaration."

"I haven't really, although I intend to. I called on Saturday and found Elizabeth alone in the garden. I don't quite know how it happened, Edward, but we were talking, and I told her that once my affairs were settled, I intended to approach her mother. Elizabeth was...was wonderful. I swear I never meant to behave improperly, but if you had seen the way she looked at me. Only a man of iron could have resisted kissing her. And that's when Lady Fairchild saw us."

"Oh, Lord, the fat's in the fire, then. Aunt Amelia is whisking Lizzie off to Harrogate tomorrow, and you are persona non grata."

"I never expected Lady Fairchild to receive me with open arms, but surely I'm not that ineligible? I would have thought my fortune—"

"Aunt Amelia wants a fortune and a title. She won't allow Lizzie to throw herself away on a nobody—I beg your pardon, Richard, of course you're not a nobody, but you know what I mean."

"Unfortunately, yes. But what of the great-aunt? I rather thought she championed my cause. Won't she do anything for us?"

"Lizzie said Aunt Horatia's behaving strangely, even for her. She's been wandering round the house muttering something or other about bad blood. When Lizzie told her what happened, all she would say was that Lizzie should do as her mother bids her. You didn't have a turn-up with the old girl, did you?"

"No, she was resting when I saw Elizabeth. I had rather counted on her support. Is she going to Harrogate, as well?"

"Not right away. Lizzie said she won't be rushed into packing. She's to follow them, travelling in style, if I know Aunt Horatia. This brandy is excellent, by the way."

"Don't drink too heavily. I did, and had a hell of a head the next morning. Edward, will you do me a favour?"

"Of course—name it."

"After Lady Fairchild leaves, will you see the great-aunt? Try to find out how she feels?"

"I'll try, but the old girl's not likely to confide in me."

"Just try. It's important to me, Edward. I think I can pacify Lady Fairchild eventually, but it would mean a lot to have the great-aunt's support. And if you have the opportunity, let Elizabeth know I won't be far away. I plan to leave for York Friday morning, and if you would care to come with me, I'd be glad of your company. I doubt I'll be away for more than a week or two."

"Capital notion. Mother's been talking about sending me North again. What are we going to do? Hunt down that castle of yours?"

"Abbey. I need to see what has to be done to restore it. Poor old house is probably in ruins. I warn you, we may not even have a place to stay."

"I'll chance it. I don't like the way Mother's been eyeing me lately. She's got some daft notion in her head, or I'll eat my hat. Stared at me all through dinner tonight."

"Why? I thought you'd reformed. Have you been out gambling and drinking again?"

"Hardly. What with keeping an eye on Lady Weymouth, I've scarce a minute to myself. That girl's got more tricks up her sleeve than Wellington. And then she sits there at dinner looking as innocent as a babe. You should have seen her this evening."

"She was at dinner tonight?"

"Lord, yes. The whole contingent of them. Lord and Lady Coltraine, Countess Wrexham, Lord—"

"But Victoria, she was there? How did she look?"

"Beautiful—she always does. All that black hair, and a white gown that was cut—"

"Edward, I just saw her on Saturday. Her face was badly bruised, and yet you tell me she was at dinner..."

His friend shook his head. "I told you, she's got more tricks than a snake charmer. Playing on your sympathy, no doubt. Did you get a close look at her bruises?"

"We were standing fairly close, but she only lifted her veil for a moment. Her cheek was black and blue, and it looked as though someone had struck her cruelly."

"There was no sign of a bruise when we sat down to dinner tonight, nor last night either. Could it have been artificial—you know, as they use on the stage?"

"It's possible, I suppose. Or perhaps she was able to cover the bruise with creams and powder. From what she told me, this is not the first time her husband has struck her."

"Richard, don't be so gullible. I've watched her and Weymouth, and I'll wager anything you like that he would never lay a hand on her. She's making game of you."

"I don't know, Edward. She must know that you would tell me..." His words trailed off as he recalled Victoria's insistence that he not say anything to Edward. "But if she were having me on, what would be the point?"

"What did she tell you?"

"She wants my help in leaving Weymouth. Victoria said he is so jealous that he flies into a rage if she looks at another man. I told her I'd arrange for a safe place for her to stay, and solicitors to file a bill of divorcement."

"I'm surprised she didn't try to convince you to run off with her. Then Weymouth would have to file for divorce, and you'd be honour bound to marry her. If that's not it, then perhaps she's just using you to throw her husband off the scent. She's definitely seeing someone else."

Richard stirred uneasily. He heard Victoria's voice, saying softly, *"With you I would go anywhere. We could even go back to India."* Was he gullible? Was Victoria trying to entrap him? He could not allow her to jeopardize his plans. "What have you found out?"

"Only that she's meeting someone secretly, and she goes to great lengths not to be discovered. Dawes and I followed her yesterday. She had Findley drive her to Russell Street to visit with her friend, Mrs. Gilderman. She must have told Findley to come back for her in a few hours, because he left at once. Lady Weymouth went in, and came back out in less than ten minutes. She waved a hackney down, and Dawes and I were able to follow her to the Park."

"And?" Richard prompted.

"And that's where we lost her. The only thing I can figure is that she must have got out when her carriage rounded a bend in the road. We followed the carriage to the North Gate before we found it was empty."

"And no sign of her in the Park?"

"None. We circled back, but she was gone. It was arranged, Richard. It had to be. Someone was there with a carriage, just waiting. She must suspect she's being followed, but it's odd—she didn't go to those lengths when she met you on Saturday. Dawes said she went straight to the modiste's. Of course I'd told him what to expect, so he didn't have any trouble tagging after her. Tonight may be a different tale, however. Dawes will be watching her like a hawk, but I fear he's not clever enough for Lady Weymouth.''

"What about the other man you thought was following her? Have you seen him again?''

"It's possible. There's a strange fellow been loitering about the Square, and I thought I caught a glimpse of him in the Park, but I couldn't swear to it. Do you think Weymouth has someone watching her?''

"The lady thinks so, or so she says, but in view of what you've told me, I'm not so certain. I wish I knew what to do, Edward. If Victoria is really being abused by her husband, I'd be seven kinds of a cad not to help her. But if she is playing off her games with me—what about her dresser? Has Dawes learned anything more from her?''

"Nothing," he said, shaking his head in disgust. "I think Dawes pressed her too hard, and she became suspicious. She refuses to talk about her mistress.''

"Damn. What of the other servants? Has there been any talk of arguments between Lord and Lady Weymouth?''

"Arguments, certainly. But if you can credit what the second housemaid says, it's Lord Weymouth that's being abused. Your Victoria, according to her, has the devil's own temper, and doesn't hesitate to rip up at anyone who displeases her, including her husband.''

"To be honest, that sounds more like the Victoria I remember from India. Even when I was infatuated with her, I was aware that she could be rather selfish. Not that she didn't have cause. She was there with her uncle and his family. Her cousins were dressed in the latest, most elegant styles, and poor Victoria had only their outdated cast-offs. But she was still the centre of attention. It didn't matter what she wore—she would have been beautiful in sackcloth, and I wasn't the only one to think so. She had every young man within miles at her beck and call.''

"That must have galled her cousins."

"It did, and Victoria gloried in it. One could hardly blame her, but it was deuced uncomfortable. If one of her admirers so much as spoke a kind word to another girl, Victoria wouldn't speak to him for the rest of the evening."

"How charming."

"She tried it on me a few times, and we argued about it, as you can imagine. But then she'd get tears in those lovely eyes, and tell me she behaved badly only because she feared losing me. Her cousins had so much more to offer, she said. And she'd look so vulnerable and hurt that it was impossible not to forgive her."

"What poppycock. And you were green enough to fall for it?"

Richard nodded. "At least for a time. Towards the end, I found it harder to make excuses for her, and to say the truth, I think I was rather secretly relieved when she chose Weymouth."

"Any man of sense would be. She might be beautiful on the outside, but that one is pure meanness inside."

"Perhaps. Still, much of the blame can be laid on her upbringing, and Victoria can be enchanting when she chooses. And there were instances when she was exceedingly kind, especially to children."

"If you are serious in your intentions towards my cousin, then you had best forget about Lady Weymouth, enchanting or no."

"I give you my word, Edward, that all I shall do is provide Victoria with a house and solicitors. No more than any friend would do."

"Well, all the same, I wouldn't tell Lizzie. She don't like Lady Weymouth as it is, and I doubt she'd understand why you feel you have to help her. Not sure I understand it myself."

"Surely you can see that I can't just turn my back on her—not when she could be in trouble, and she's asked for my help."

A loud crash sounded in the hall, distracting both men.

"What the devil?" Richard stood and strode round the desk. He stopped abruptly as the door to the library crashed inward, and a man reeling off balance staggered and fell to his knees.

It took Richard a second to recognize Lord Weymouth's cherubic features beneath a white wig, sadly askew over one eye.

Philbin's ponderous form filled the doorway, his face red with exertion. "I'm sorry, sir. I tried to keep him from barging in on you, but he shoved me out of the way." He paused to gain his breath, and then added petulantly, "He broke Caesar's head, too. It's scattered all over the hall. I shudder to think what Lord Batterton will say."

"It's all right, Philbin. Apparently Lord Weymouth has had a trifle too much to drink. You may go."

Philbin sniffed audibly before quietly closing the door, and Lord Edward resumed his seat, amusement lighting his eyes.

"I envy you, Richard. You have the sort of house where acquaintances must always feel free to just *drop in.*"

Richard shot him a dark look, but Edward was unabashed.

"And poor Caesar—beheaded in your hall. 'O mighty Caesar! dost thou lie so low? Et tu, Brute!'"

"Cut line, Edward. Can't you see that Weymouth is obviously troubled. This is no time for your wit."

"Of course not. One can see that this is a serious business. Perhaps he has come to *bury* Caesar?"

Richard ignored his idiotic grin and offered his hand to Weymouth, but the smaller man ignored it. Richard turned his back on the man, thinking to save him some shred of dignity, and returned to his desk, shaking his head at Edward.

Weymouth managed to regain his feet, pulling his waistcoat down and shoving his wig up. His stockings were badly wrinkled, and one had a long rent at the knee. His coat was heavily stained and his stock was twisted round the pudgy neck and over the coat. Richard couldn't help smiling at his disarray, but the smile rapidly disappeared as Weymouth pulled out a long-handled duelling pistol, waving it wildly at Richard.

"Laugh at me, will you? We'll see who gets buried."

CHAPTER NINE

LORD WEYMOUTH levelled the gun at Richard, and then, seeing Edward start to rise, swung wildly in his direction. "Stay where you are, or I'll put a bullet through your pretty curls." He watched, a mad light in his eyes, as Edward slowly sank into his chair.

Richard, his hands on the desk in front of him, and sweat running down his arms, tried to speak quietly and calmly. "Lord Weymouth, whatever reason you may have for—"

"Where is she? I know she's here—where have you got her hidden?" His voice rose, almost breaking. "Victoria!" he screamed loudly, his head swivelling left and right.

Edward was close enough to make a dive for the pistol, but Richard, reading his thoughts, shook his head. He spoke quietly, almost soothingly. "Your wife is not here, Weymouth. She has never been in this house."

"Don't lie to me, Danvers. I know she's here and I'm not leaving without her." He waved the gun again, but his hand was shaking, and there was less conviction in his voice.

Richard deliberately seated himself. "Then you are in for a long wait, sir. I tell you again your wife is not here, nor have I seen or spoken with her this evening. I give you my word."

Weymouth stared at him, doubt creeping into his eyes, and his lips began to tremble. "I...I was so sure...she said she was going to bed early. Had a headache. But then I checked, and she wasn't in her room. I was sure..."

"Give me the gun and then we'll talk."

Weymouth took a step forward, his hand trembling badly. Before he could place the pistol on the desk, the door crashed open again, and he spun round, his back to Richard and Edward. Roscoe stood in the open doorway like a cocky bantam rooster with one of Richard's duelling pistols in each hand.

"You best be laying that shooter down nice and easy like, sir. These pop guns are Mr. Danvers's, and I ain't never fired 'em, but chances are even if you fired, I could still get a hit in."

"Roscoe, did you load those pistols?" Richard asked urgently.

"Of course I did. Wouldn't do much good holding empty shooters on a man. Now—"

"Roscoe, listen to me. I don't want you interfering. Lay those pistols down as gently as possible. They both have hair-triggers."

"But, sir, what about—"

"I'm giving you an order, Roscoe. Lay those pistols down *now*."

"Yes, sir," Roscoe muttered, and tried to edge closer to the desk. At least he could place the guns near Richard. He kept his eyes warily on Weymouth and didn't see the footstool directly in his path.

Richard yelled a warning, but it was too late. Roscoe tumbled forward and both pistols discharged. Richard ducked beneath the desk, and Edward dived for the floor. The only one left standing was Weymouth, who looked round him in astonishment.

The awesome sound of the shots reverberated through the room, followed by an ominous silence. Richard peered over the edge of the desk, trying to see through the haze of smoke. Weymouth stood in the centre of the room, his own gun lowered, tears running down his face.

"Roscoe? Edward? Are you all right?"

"No harm here," Edward announced, rising awkwardly and brushing at his coat.

Roscoe rose more slowly, red faced and cowed. "I never meant to set 'em off, sir. I didn't see—"

"We'll discuss it later," Richard interrupted, his voice cold. "For now, bring the guns here, and then you may leave, and close the door after you. Edward, would you pull up that chair for Weymouth before he passes out, and I'll get the brandy?"

The servants milling in the hall were dispersed as Roscoe left, and a few minutes later order, of a sort, was restored. Richard looked round ruefully. A large portrait of a sea-going captain hung over the fireplace. The captain no longer had a face. The other bullet had shattered a window near the terrace. The damage, considering what might have been, was relatively minor.

Edward readily accepted the proffered glass, but Richard had to place one in Weymouth's hand, and half-force him to drink it. He sputtered and coughed as the fiery liquid went down his throat, but some colour returned to his face, and after a moment he was able to hold the glass.

Richard returned to his own chair behind the desk, and thankfully took a sip of brandy. His eyes met Edward's over the glass, and suddenly the two men exploded into laughter.

"Lord save me from over-zealous servants," Edward said, wiping at his eyes. "Did you see the way he stood in the door? I shall have to take better care of you, Richard, or your valet will have my head as a full measure of revenge."

Richard smiled, but sobered again as he faced Weymouth. "You shall have to forgive my valet, sir. I know you never intended to use that pistol, but Roscoe acted in the belief that he was protecting me."

"It was because of him," Weymouth muttered.

"I beg your pardon?"

"Him. That valet of yours. I've seen him hanging round the square this past week. Just waiting for Vickie to come out. I knew he was your man. Probably carrying messages to you. She may not be here now, but you can't deny—"

"I do deny it. If my valet was watching Lady Weymouth, it was not on my orders, and certainly without my knowledge."

Lord Weymouth wanted to believe him, but he had seen the man with his own eyes, and on several different occasions. "Then how do you explain it? Why else would he hang about?"

Richard chose his words carefully. "Roscoe has been with me since I was ten years old. In some ways, he still regards me as a little boy in need of his help. He was with me in India when I became . . . infatuated with Victoria. When he learned that she was in London, I'm afraid he feared I might once again become enamoured of her, sir. I don't know how to put this delicately, but I believe he and my groom took it upon themselves to watch Victoria in hopes that she would do something to discredit her claim on my friendship."

"Friendship?" The heavy jowls quivered in disbelief.

Richard nodded. "I cared, once, very deeply for Victoria. If she needs my help now, I would give it gladly, but only, I assure you, in friendship."

"Why should she need *your* help? I'm her husband. I can give her anything she wants," Weymouth said, his voice rising.

Richard shifted uncomfortably, and caught a devilish grin from Edward. "Perhaps that is something you should discuss with your wife, sir. I can only tell you that Victoria pleaded with me to help her."

"Bah! This is nonsense. She has everything a woman could want, and then some." His eyes fell on Edward, and he shifted his attack. "If not Danvers, then perhaps it's you she's been seeing. Don't think I haven't noticed the way you stare at her and follow her about."

Edward drew himself up, and for a brief second, Weymouth had the uncomfortable feeling that it was the duke himself answering.

"If I stared at your wife, sir, it was only because I, too, like Richard's servants, am desirous of protecting him. Frankly, Weymouth, I don't trust your wife. And after your performance this evening, I don't scruple to tell you that I know she is seeing someone secretly, and that person is neither Richard nor myself."

Richard tensed, ready to interfere, but Weymouth sat stricken. His air of belligerence vanished, and once more tears streamed from his eyes. He was stripped of all pride, and sobbed heavily, "I can't bear it, if she leaves me. God help me, I love her more than life itself."

Edward, feeling slightly ashamed, turned away. Richard sought for words to comfort the older man. "Talk to Victoria, tell her how you feel."

"I've tried. I can't get the words out. I choke up. All I can do is give her money. Buy her things. I thought it was enough.... She's so beautiful, I always knew someone would take her away from me."

"Victoria told me you're jealous of every man she looks at."

He shook his head, gesturing widely with his hands, "I can't help it. I'm always afraid... afraid she'll leave."

"Have you ever tried to stop her?" The words came out like a whip lash.

"Stop her? How? If she wants to go, what can I do?"

"Have you ever struck her?" Weymouth looked appalled, and Richard added softly, "I can understand if in a rage of jealousy—"

"Never! How can you even suggest such a thing? Don't you understand? Can't you see how much I love her, worship her? How could you ever think I would strike her? Mark her beauty?" He was on his feet, leaning over the desk, determined to make Richard understand.

"Sit down, Lord Weymouth. I apologize for distressing you, but it was something I had to ask. You see, Victoria told me you beat her, and when I saw her on Saturday, she had a bruise on her face, below the right eye."

Weymouth was incredulous. "It's not possible... you're lying. She would never say such a thing."

Richard remained silent, and Weymouth, realizing the insult he had offered, retracted slightly. "You must have misunderstood her... she can't have meant—she knows I'd never harm her."

"You must talk with her, Weymouth. I promised Victoria I'd find a house for her, and I intended to give her the lease on Thursday. I'll hold off, at least until I come back from Yorkshire, since she doesn't seem to be in any immediate danger. But I want your word that you'll at least try to talk the matter over with her."

Weymouth nodded morosely, confused and uncertain now. He'd been so sure that Victoria was having an affair with Richard. That, at least, he could have understood. She'd been half in love with the younger man when he'd met her. And then so proud when she'd chosen to wed him instead of Richard. Now he didn't know what to believe, and he sat silently in his chair, lost in his thoughts.

Richard approached him and gently helped him to his feet. "I think you should go home now. Try to get some sleep, and talk to your wife tomorrow. Perhaps matters are not as bleak as you believe."

Lord Weymouth allowed himself to be led quietly from the room, and Richard saw him safely to his carriage. When he returned, he found Edward studying the portrait of the Captain.

"Not much left of the old fellow. Shouldn't think you could have it restored. How will you explain it to Lord Batterton?"

"The truth, of course."

"He'll never believe it. Wouldn't have believed it myself, if I hadn't seen it. Tell me, Richard, did you attract this much trouble in India?"

Richard smiled wryly, thinking of the orderly, uneventful life he'd lived in Josiah's house. "No, although I was frequently told that I should visit England because it's so much more civilized."

IRONICALLY, RICHARD recalled his words the following evening when Lord Demeral joined him for dinner. Bribery had been the order of the day in India, where treaties were made and broken with ease. Trust was not a commodity found in abundance in Calcutta. Still, Richard preferred the double-dealings of the nawabs and Sikhs to the smooth-face perfidy of men like Demeral.

The older man barely made a pretence of enjoying the sumptuous repast Richard's chef had prepared. He was too anxious for their card game to linger over the roasted pheasant or the rack of lamb so deliciously prepared. To his host's offer of an after-dinner brandy, Demeral suggested they retire to the salon and drink it while they played.

Richard agreed and led the way. He excused himself for a few minutes and quietly instructed Philbin to post a footman in the room. He wanted the glasses kept full throughout the evening. He returned to the table and engaged Demeral in light conversation while the cards were dealt. At first, Demeral barely answered, his concentration solely on the game. But as the pile of markers in front of him grew, and the level of the decanter decreased, he became more talkative.

Richard played skilfully, winning on small bets and losing heavily on larger ones while he brought the conversation round to the various clubs of London. He hoped to induce Demeral to speak about White's, since it was there he'd lost his fortune.

"Perhaps you can advise me, Lord Demeral. Salford is willing to put my name up at several clubs. He, of course, belongs to them all, but one will be sufficient for me. Do you recommend White's or Brooks's?" Richard played his king, neatly turning down the ace in his hand, and watched while Demeral happily took the hand.

"Oh, Brooks's, if you've a choice. Even the Regent favours it, though it's more difficult to be elected there than at White's."

"So I've heard. I understand almost anyone with funds enough can get in at White's," Richard murmured, hoping to bring the conversation round to Pembroke.

Demeral, busy dealing the cards, did not take the hint. "Quite. Brooks's, on the other hand, is more selective. Have you heard the tale of Fighting Fitzgerald?"

"I don't believe so," Richard said, resigned.

"Of course it was a good many years ago, but the story goes this George Fitzgerald was a notable duellist, and because of the men he'd killed, he was kept out of most of the clubs. Well, one day he proposed to this admiral that he put his name forward for Brooks's. Admiral Keith agreed, you see, because it was either that or meet him on the field."

"Hardly a choice."

"Well, the admiral put his name up, and then black-balled him, of course. But when old Brooks told Fitzgerald that he'd been blackballed, the Irishman tells him obviously a mistake was made, and demands they elect him again. This time, they tell him, there were *two* black balls in the ballot box. Fitzgerald declares there must be two mistakes, then, and pushing past old Brooks goes upstairs and questions each of the members. Of course, they all denied blackballing him, and he declares that he knew it was all a mistake, and here he was elected unanimously."

"Then it's not so difficult after all to be elected to Brooks's, if one has enough gall," Richard said with a laugh.

"Didn't do him no good," Demeral said, trouncing on a ten of hearts. "The members sent him to Coventry. Wouldn't no one talk to him. Can't force yourself on the ton. If you're an outcast, you're an outcast." His words were beginning to be slurred, and Richard decided more direct measures would have to be taken.

"Like Lord Pembroke? I understand there was some sort of scandal, and he's no longer received in Polite Society."

For a brief instant, Demeral's dark eyes seemed to sharpen as he looked across at Richard. "Why do you bring his name up?"

"Only because you mentioned you lost your fortune to him, and Salford said something about him being an outcast."

Demeral was diverted again as the ace of hearts turned up, and he took the hand easily. The footman refilled his glass, and after a sip, he replied easily. "Haven't seen Pembroke in six or seven years. Wasn't long after he stripped me of my inheritance that he was stripped of everything himself. Oh, not his fortune. He still has that. But it doesn't do him much good. He ran off with another man's wife. Took her to his country seat up North, and lived openly with her, too. And her a lady. No one received them after that. It was the talk of the Town for a while. Her husband refused to divorce her, but I heard he died a few years back, and old Pembroke finally married the lady."

"He belonged to White's, I believe you said. Hardly a recommendation for that club."

"Oh, he was pretty well thought of when he was a member. Fooled the lot of them, but not me. I saw through him, right enough."

"And yet, you played against him?"

"Challenged me at White's. There wasn't nothing else I could do. It was play or be ostracized."

"Do you think he cheated?"

Again the black eyes focused sharply. "Are you deliberately trying to provoke me, Mr. Danvers?"

"No, of course not. Why should you think so?" Richard asked, doing his best to look nonchalant.

Demeral raked in the markers. Obviously, the card game was over, and he'd won a tidy sum. The brandy, too, had a mellowing effect, and he almost smiled at the innocence of Danvers.

"You'll hear the story, sooner or later, so I might as well be the one to tell you. It was seven years ago, and I was only a mite older than you. I had a reputation, Mr. Danvers, for being clever at cards. In point of fact, my inheritance was meager, and it was my skill at cards which enabled me to command the most elegant mode of life. I was, shall we say, fortunate, and won repeatedly. It was not remarked on much, until a certain Mr. Philip Gerant came up to London."

He paused, a reminiscent look in his eyes, and Richard motioned to the footman to fill his glass. Demeral hardly noticed.

"Mr. Gerant had a tidy fortune, and it was his first visit to London. A friend brought him along to White's one evening when I was there. Perhaps he'd had too much to drink, or perhaps he overestimated his skill. At any rate, before the evening was done, I owned his estate. Mr. Gerant left the club somewhat dazed. No one saw him for several days, and it was his friend, Mr. Gifford, who finally found him. Gerant had died in his rooms. Blew his head off with a duelling pistol."

"Lord, you must have—"

"Felt badly? No. If you can't afford to pay, you shouldn't play. That's my motto. However, there were others who took a dim view of the affair. Lord Pembroke was one. Nothing was said to my face, of course.

Just whispers behind my back. No one cut me direct, but I wasn't asked anywhere, and conversations had a way of ceasing when I entered a room. Pembroke was behind it all."

"How could you know that?"

"He challenged me a week later. Ironically, we played at the same table in White's. And ironically, he won everything. I still don't know how he did it, although my luck was certainly out that night. Of course, all the members were there, watching and hoping. They cheered him on. They wanted me to lose."

"I'm sorry, Lord Demeral. I didn't mean to—"

"I survived, Danvers. I always will. And I didn't whine about losing, either. I started over, and would've won my fortune back, too, if Pembroke hadn't retired. But there are others. I'll have my estates back one day, and more."

Richard believed him. Some other young man would come up to Town and have the misfortune to run into Demeral. Richard knew he'd been marking the cards all night, but much good that knowledge would do anyone. The unfortunate young man would have the choice of losing gracefully, or facing Demeral on the green. He felt rather sick at heart and looked with distaste at his guest.

Demeral, sensing his feelings, gathered up his cards and markers. "I don't know why you asked me here, Danvers, nor much care. But if it's Pembroke you're after, I suggest you tread softly. He's a wily old bird, and not above a trick or two of his own. Still, I wouldn't mind evening the score between us a bit. If you find yourself in need of help, just send me word."

Richard showed him out without commenting either way. The thought of Demeral as an ally was repugnant. He'd find a way to approach Pembroke without his help, of that he was certain. He paused at the door of the salon, but the air was heavy with the smell of smoke, and he turned towards the library instead.

None of the books which Richard looked at held any interest for him, and he was about to retire to his rooms when Philbin knocked discreetly.

"Excuse me, sir, but His Grace, the Duke of Cardiff, wishes a word with you."

Richard looked up surprised. He'd not exchanged more than a half-dozen words with the duke when he was a guest in his home. He rose quickly. "Your Grace, is Lord Edward—"

"My son is fine, in so far as I know. The reason for this late visit has nothing to do with him. It's business with you, *my lord,* which brings me here."

Richard's eyes studied him, but the duke gave nothing away. "You know who I am, then?"

"I realized it today. I'm afraid I didn't connect the name until I received a dispatch from Calcutta informing me of your departure."

"Why should my movements be of any concern to you?"

"My dear boy, you have been watched closely ever since it became apparent that you would be Danvers's heir."

"I'm afraid I still don't understand, Your Grace."

"If we might be seated?" The duke gestured, and Richard belatedly offered him a chair, and a drink, as well. When they were settled, with cognac before them, the duke continued. "Surely, you must realize the delicate situation which exists in India? Why, the papers have been full of it, and the Houses debate constantly over the East India Trading Company."

"I'm aware of that, of course, but neither my stepfather nor I have anything to do with the company."

"Not directly, perhaps, but you wield a great deal of power in Calcutta. Your influence with the nawabs has never been underestimated, and we know that even the Governor-General has frequently sought your advice on internal affairs."

"I fear you flatter me, but even were such the case, why should that interest you personally?"

"Anything which might change the balance of power in India interests me. I am on the Board of Control for the affairs of the East India Company. I have to make decisions every day and am hampered by the lack of any first-hand information. Information which is not prejudicial. The reason various guests are even now at my home has to do with India, and decisions which I must make. I had thought Weymouth might help, but his grasp of the political situation there is...to say the least, inadequate."

"Do you think that my grasp is any better?"

"You lived there, Richard, for years. You've seen the struggles for control, the drastic changes. Between you and Josiah, you must've known them all—Cornwallis, Wellesley, Lord Minto. Your observations could be invaluable to me."

"I don't fancy that my opinions would find favour with a supporter of the Company, Your Grace. Edward has already cautioned me not to mention how poorly the Prince Regent is thought of in India."

"My concern, sir, is not the Company, or indeed any individual, but England itself. Anything you say to me will be fairly evaluated—and of course held in strict confidence."

"Then I am at your disposal. What is it you wish to know?"

"Lord, if only I'd known who you were when you were a guest in my house. The hours I've wasted. And there's not much time left. The board must reach a decision soon." He took a sip of the cognac, and then fired question after question at Richard. "What do you know of Metcalfe? Elphinstone? Lord Moira? Would it be worthwhile for England if the Company seized control of Java from the Dutch?"

The questions went on for hours. The duke was astute and quick to grasp the finer nuances of Richard's remarks. He even smiled, once, when Richard spoke scathingly of Sir Arthur Wellesley.

"You do know that Wellesley is considered something of a hero here? Although his brother, Richard, was brought up on charges in the House of Commons for abuse of office. Fox and the Prince Regent were behind that."

"They should have charged Sir Arthur, as well. In the last battle he led, at Assaye—a battle that lasted for only three hours—almost a thousand British soldiers were killed, and well over 1,800 wounded. It was appalling."

"Yes, I believe he said something to that effect in his dispatch, although he considered the battle worth it. Assaye put the Company in solid control of India."

"And that is the whole question, isn't it, Your Grace? Is the Company in India to expand trade, or to act as sovereign ruler of that country?"

"I would be much interested in your opinion, Richard."

"I am hardly less prejudiced than some of your other advisers. I have long felt the Company exceeded its authority, especially under Wellesley. The cost must have been astronomical, not only in human lives but economically. The trade is there, and other than the lust for personal riches and advancement, there is no need for the Company to rule India. In fact, I personally hope the Crown will see fit to end the monopoly on trade the Company holds."

The duke was silent for a moment. "I say this for your ears alone, Richard, but the time is coming. If we are successful, I look to see the monopoly ended within a year or two. It might be wise to sell out your holdings in Calcutta."

"Thank you, Your Grace. I've been considering doing just that, and I'm honoured by your confidence."

"It will mean a fight. Pitt and Granville supported Wellesley's expansionist policy, and they'll do everything they can to stop me. Would you be willing to speak before a committee, if I need you?"

"Certainly, Your Grace, as Richard Danvers, if you permit."

The duke nodded, and then stood, offering Richard his hand. "If that is your wish, sir. However, I hope it won't be long before you take your rightful place as Lord St. Symington. England needs men like you."

"Thank you," Richard said quietly, moved by the duke's sincerity.

"It is I who owe you thanks. I deeply appreciate your patience with my endless questions. And one other thing, Richard. Should you chance to speak with Amelia Fairchild, you may say that I, as head of the family, give full approval to a match between you and Elizabeth."

Richard caught the twinkle in his eyes, and openly grinned as the Duke of Cardiff took his leave.

CHAPTER TEN

THURSDAY DAWNED BRIGHT and sunny, and although it was still cold, it seemed a perfect day for a trip out of London. Richard might have been a trifle testy when Roscoe woke him at an early hour, but once he was on the open road, his spirit was soon restored. Roscoe, fearful of a long lecture from his master, had elected to ride outside with Kirby, and Richard consequently had the huge carriage to himself.

He settled into the luxurious cushions with a sigh of relief. So much had happened during the past few days that he needed this interlude to put his thoughts in order. And the carriage drive to and from Runnymede would likely be his only opportunity for solitude. Tomorrow morning he and Lord Edward would set forth for the Abbey. Richard judged that if they took the North Road to York, and then turned southwest through Harrogate, they should reach the Abbey sometime on Saturday afternoon.

Weycross Abbey. It would be the first time he saw his home in almost fifteen years. He alternated between exultant feelings of anticipation and dread that the home he loved so dearly would be in ruins. The Abbey was his only link to his childhood now that both his parents were dead. Except for Chilly. He smiled, thinking of his old nurse, wondering how much she had changed with the years, and hoping she would still be the same safe, dependable Chilly. She had comforted the small boy frequently, bandaging his cuts and nursing his bruises. And it was to Chilly the small boy had turned when Lady St. Symington had locked herself in her rooms—refusing to see anyone, not even her son—for days on end.

Disturbed by his memories, Richard glanced out the window. They were passing Windsor, and he saw the great castle poised on the edge of the cliff overlooking the Thames. Roscoe had reported Runnymede lay just south of Windsor, and Richard, anxious now, kept a look-out for his first glimpse of the town. Still, it was almost a full hour before the carriage slowed its pace. They passed through a narrow street, with tall stands of oaks on the right, and market buildings on the left. Leaving the town behind, Kirby turned the team to the right and minutes later halted them before a tidy wood cottage. Just the sort of place where he pictured Chilly living. Roses climbed a trellis on one side of the entrance, and a large tub of pansies adorned the other.

He had just stepped from the carriage when a woman of more than ample girth appeared in the doorway. Her head was wreathed with white hair, and a wide smile creased the round, pudgy face with a hundred wrinkles. Chilly was almost double the size Richard remembered, but he had no difficulty recognizing her. The tiny blue eyes, although almost lost in the folds of her face, still twinkled merrily.

"Lordy, is that you Master Richard? I've been on the watch for you ever since I got Lady Sewell's note, but I can scarce credit my eyes. Who would have thought that scrawny little boy would grow into such a fine, handsome man?"

She had no time to say more. Richard, reverting to nine-year-old status, stepped swiftly forward and enveloped her in a crushing hug.

"Chilly, oh, Chilly, it's so good to see you. You haven't changed a bit."

"Go on with you, Master Richard," she scolded, drawing back. "Laying the butter on a mite thick, you be. Now let me look at you." She stood, arms akimbo, waiting for Richard to turn for her inspection. He complied, while Roscoe and Kirby watched from the box, grinning their approval.

"Aye, it's a handsome man you are, and will be driving the ladies to foolishness, I don't doubt." The eyes clouded over, and Mrs. Chiltern dabbed at them with a corner of her apron. "I thought I'd never see you again, you stayed in that heathen country so long. I doubt Lady Anne would have had the courage to send you away if she had known how many years it'd be before you remembered where your home was."

Richard had no desire to discuss his mother in front of Roscoe and Kirby and, after introducing them hastily, sent them to the nearest inn to quench their thirst. He followed his old nurse into the tiny cottage where she proudly installed him in the best chair in the front room, before bustling off to the kitchen to produce a lavish tea.

Enticing aromas wafted across the room, and the smell of fresh baked bread instantly transformed Richard back to his childhood. Memories assailed him of a six-year-old boy sitting in just such a chair, and waiting for Chilly to soothe his hurt with hot chocolate and cakes.

Young Richard had sat well back in the chair, his chubby little legs too short to reach the floor, and sniffled quietly. His father had made it quite clear what he thought of young boys who cried, and the lad struggled manfully to hold back his tears.

He surreptitiously wiped his eyes on the sleeve of his jacket, and hiccoughed as a sob escaped him. His mother had locked herself in her room for the past three days and refused to see him. That afternoon he had gone, as was his usual custom, to take tea with her, but again her door was locked. Richard had stood against it, whining pitifully to be admitted. Her maid opened the door at last, but only a crack, and only to tell the little boy he was to take his tea with Mrs. Chiltern. The door had shut firmly before he could protest, and a footman had appeared to escort him to the nursery.

Chilly, after one look at the woebegone face, had hugged him tightly. He was scared to death, poor mite, and she did her best to reassure him.

"But why can't I see Mama, Chilly?"

"Your mama just doesn't feel up to seeing anyone, not even you. Now, don't be fretting. In another day or two, she'll be herself again, and you'll be having your tea with her, and leaving me all alone."

Young Richard had not been diverted. While his nurse had bustled about preparing his tea, the boy had sat in the oversize chair, struggling with his thoughts. He remembered Mrs. Newhouse, their agent's wife. She had gone to sleep, and never woke up. Richard had seen her, sleeping in her wooden box at the chapel, and then they had closed the lid, and put her in the ground. The fear that they might do the same thing to his mama lay like a cold stone in his stomach.

When Chilly finally placed the tea tray before him, he asked again why he couldn't see his mama. She had no answer, and sought to distract him with chocolate and cakes. His fears had gradually lessened under her loving kindness, and when, two days later, he rejoined his mama for tea, the boy blocked the memory from his mind.

There were other incidents as the years passed, and Richard grew accustomed to his mother's isolation for days at a time. He no longer trembled with fear, but his questions still went unanswered. When he was older he speculated on the possible reasons for his mother's strange behaviour. The episodes with her always coincided with his father's disappearance from the house for several weeks, and Richard wondered if his mother had an overfondness for drink.

Chilly's heavy tread and a plate of sweet-smelling cakes waved beneath his nose recalled him to the present. But the questions from his childhood still lingered, and Richard resolved to see if Chilly would at last provide him with some answers. He waited till she poured the tea and settled herself comfortably.

"Lady Sewell gave me your direction, Chilly. She bade me to ask you about my parents. I've been sitting here reminiscing, remembering those times when you gave me tea. Chilly, what was wrong with my mother? Why did she lock herself in her rooms and then finally send me as far away as she could?"

The old woman studied him and then nodded to herself, as if coming to a decision. "I suppose you're old enough now to understand...and you've a right to know. But in the old days, well, Lady Anne swore us all to secrecy. Mind you, I don't say she was in the right of it, but she did it for your own good. Your innocence was your protection—that's what she always told us."

Richard's hand gripped the tea saucer tightly. He felt an uncomfortable sensation in his stomach, a dread of what he was about to hear. Still, he forced himself to ask, "Protection from what, Chilly?"

"Your father, may God have mercy on his soul." She looked him straight in the eye. "I don't hold none with speaking ill of the dead, Master Richard, but your father was an evil man. The Good Book says the memory of the just is blessed, but the name of the wicked shall rot. And though it pains me to tell you so, your father was a wicked man."

Richard swallowed the bile which rose in his throat. He wanted to leave—leave quickly before he heard words which could never be unsaid. Chilly didn't understand. Didn't realize what she was saying. Richard struggled to deny her words, but as he stared at the old woman before him, her eyes sad and troubled, he knew she believed what she was saying, and that he would have to stay and hear her story.

"Your mother was the sweetest, kindest, most gentle soul that ever trod this earth. And pretty, too. She went to St. Symington full of innocence and love. I wish you could have seen her, Master Richard, in those early days. Long blond curls trailing down her back, and brown eyes so full of happiness and love. Everyone loved Lady Anne."

"Including my father?"

"Aye, even him. And, mayhap, that was his undoing. He weren't so bad in the beginning. But he had a weakness for the bottle, and when he was in his cups, there was no reasoning with him. He accused Lady Anne of the most vile, despicable acts. Mad with jealousy and drink driving him on. If Lady Anne so much as smiled at a guest, he accused her in front of everyone of bedding him. There were even times when he denied you were his own born, as if you weren't the spitting image of his own father."

"Perhaps he had reason for his doubts, Chilly. Surely, you weren't in a position to know definitely that... that..."

"That your sainted mother didn't cuckold him?"

He blanched at her frankness, but still struggled to retain the image he cherished of his father. "Not that, but she was beautiful. I'm sure many gentlemen must have found her attractive, and if she perhaps flirted with them? In all innocence, of course," he hastened to add.

"After the first time, when he accused her of seducing poor Lord Montford, you may be sure Lady Anne was at pains to give your father no cause for his suspicions. But it didn't matter. Even when guests were no longer received at the Abbey, he swore the poor sweet lass was meeting someone secretly. Demented, he was."

Richard took a bite of one of the small cakes so lovingly prepared for him, but it tasted like sawdust in his mouth. He strove to find some justification for his father's actions. Some plausible reason which would drive a sane man to drink and allow for jealous rages. He recalled uneasily the time his father had accused his mother of an affair with Lord Frome, and Edward Salford's disbelief at the very notion.

Mrs. Chiltern watched him. She had dearly loved this man when he was a lad, and she half-wished to protect him from the knowledge of his father's baseness. But Lady Anne deserved to have the truth known, and now he was home, it was only a matter of time before Richard would discover the whole unsavoury business. It was better it come from her.

"You asked me before, Master Richard, why your mama locked herself away. Given your father's behaviour, have you no notion?"

"None...save...I sometimes wondered if she—if she, too, had a fondness for drink?"

"After seeing what it did to your father, Lady Anne wouldn't even touch a glass of sherry." She reached a comforting hand across to him. "No, it was to spare you, Master Richard. She was afraid of what would happen if you were to see her with her face all black and blue with bruises, and swollen almost beyond recognition."

Richard shook the hand off, and stood, his eyes grown cold and the scar beneath pulsing rapidly. "What are you saying? Surely, you cannot be accusing Father of beating my mother? The very idea is outrageous. No gentleman would—"

"He was no gentleman, Master Richard, not even when he was sober, which was seldom enough near the end. He beat her half-senseless, but what she feared most was that he would one day vent his anger on you."

"Surely, if what you are saying is true, someone would have—her family would have intervened."

"He set their backs up from the first. Not one of them would set foot in the Abbey, and she wouldn't write them. She was too ashamed. The poor darling feared that she was somehow to blame. The only one she kept in correspondence with was Josiah, and the only reason St. Symington allowed her to do so was because he was half the world away."

Richard walked to the window, unable to bear hearing any more, but Chilly's voice pursued him.

"It fair broke her heart to send you away, Master Richard. I don't think I ever heard her laugh again, once you left the house. You were the only thing which made her life bearable, and when you wouldn't answer her letters, well, that don't bear speaking of."

She watched him standing before the window, his shoulders hunched forward, and knew she'd dealt him a sore blow. The chair groaned as she shifted her weight and rose to go to him.

"She never wanted you to know, Master Richard. I argued with her about you, but, bless her, she wanted you to think well of your father. She said a boy needed that."

He turned, eyes blazing. "Then why the devil are you telling me this now?"

Mrs. Chiltern stepped back involuntarily, but she held his eyes. "Only because Lady Sewell wrote that you'd some notion of avenging your father's death and harming Lord Pembroke. And he, poor man, was the only one what ever tried to help milady."

Her voice was defiant and Richard knew an urge to strike out at her. The thought shook him. Hands clenched, temper barely in check, he strode to the door and yanked it open. "I need some air. If my man comes back, have him wait."

Mrs. Chiltern watched from the window, tears in her eyes. She longed to call him back, and comfort him as she used to. But cakes and chocolate wouldn't be what the Master needed this time.

The sun was near to setting when Richard finally returned. It was not coincidence that he arrived only minutes after Kirby and Roscoe. He'd spent the past two hours in a copse at the end of the street, pacing off his fury, and on the look-out for Kirby. He appeared outwardly calm, but he made sure that there was no chance for further conversation with his old nurse. He took his leave outside the cottage, and although he allowed her to hug him, his body remained stiff and unyielding.

Roscoe shared the carriage with him, and they'd not gone above a mile before the little valet realized Richard was in one of his rare black moods. His master might try to put him off with talk of how tired he was, but Roscoe was a more knowing one than that. He studied Richard curiously. The young lord had his head thrown back and was feigning sleep, but Roscoe noted the scar beneath his eye was beating wildly. And his hands were clenched so tightly that the knuckles showed white.

The carriage hit a bump, and Richard's eyes flew open. Roscoe grinned. "Doubt you'll get much sleep with the conditions of these roads, sir. I'll wager it's right rough going when the snows come. Still, I suppose there's not enough traffic to warrant fixing 'em. They told me and Kirby at the tavern that they don't get many visitors. Your coming here must have been a high treat for your old nurse."

Richard eyed him belligerently before shifting his position and closing his eyes again. Another rut jostled the carriage, and Richard swore fluently.

Roscoe continued innocently, "Mrs. Chiltern was mighty pleased to see you, I don't doubt. The innkeeper let on as how she did a passel of shopping, more 'an she usually does in a month of Sundays. Told 'em all in town how she was fixing a fancy tea for a young gentleman. Seems like a sweet old lady."

"So she might to someone who did not know her when she had all her wits about her," Richard answered sharply. "If you are endeavouring with this inane, roundabout conversation to find out what occurred, you may save your breath. Mrs. Chiltern has grown as senile as she is fat, and nothing she had to say bears repeating."

"Senile? Now, she didn't strike me as—"

"The woman is obviously prey to delusions," Richard broke in. "She rambled on about my parents in the most maddening way until I was forced to take my leave. One cannot give credence to anything she said.''

"Ah, it's sad what age does to some. What kind of delusions, sir, if you don't mind me asking?''

Richard frowned. He didn't want to befoul his father's memory by even voicing the words, but he needed someone to agree with his judgement. Someone to tell him that, of course, the old woman was quite mad.

"She . . . she insinuated that my father used to beat my mother. Beat her badly enough that she had to lock herself in her room for days. Of course, it's totally absurd. My father was a gentleman. She must be mad to even imagine such a thing. He was a gentleman, Roscoe.''

It wouldn't pay toll to argue with him, Roscoe thought, making soothing noises. It looked like the young master was doing enough arguing with himself for the pair of 'em. He kept his thoughts to himself, merely agreeing with Richard from time to time, as he dredged up memories from his childhood. It was his father, Richard said, who first put him up on a horse. And taught him to fire a gun. Roscoe allowed him to talk, but the memories he could recount were few, and even those few seemed to somehow fall short of convincing either man of the worthiness of the old lord.

RICHARD SPENT a restless night, tormented by nightmares, the like of which he'd not suffered since he was six. It was almost a relief when Roscoe roused him at seven, reminding him they were to call for Lord Edward within the hour.

He put his mind firmly on the journey to Yorkshire. He and Edward could travel in the curricle, and Roscoe, Kirby and Dawes could follow with the luggage in the carriage. The long drive, with Edward's amusing company, would clear his mind. At the moment, his head felt as though it were packed with cotton.

Edward was not only ready when they arrived, but waiting in the carriage drive. Richard brought his curricle to a neat halt, and his friend climbed aboard with such haste that he almost slipped.

"You'll want to change your plans a bit, Richard, when I tell you what I've learned," Edward said by way of greeting. He had the smug look of one who held all the trump cards and would take pleasure in playing them one at a time.

"Don't expect me to guess. I don't believe I'm capable of putting two coherent thoughts together—not this morning. I doubt I slept above an hour the whole night."

"You do look a bit drawn," his friend conceded with scant sympathy, "but you'll perk up when I give you my news. I've found Victoria out!"

Richard was having a devilish time controlling his horses while he waited for Dawes to finish loading Edward's trunks. He checked them sharply, silently cursing the pain in his shoulder, before risking a look at Edward.

"I knew my sleuthing abilities would pay off. Take Kensington Road west till we reach the Gardens. I'll direct you from there. It gets a bit tricky, but I drew a map so I could find the place again."

"What place?" Richard demanded, exasperation creeping into his voice. "And why should we go to Kensington Gardens when we should be heading north?"

"Tsk, tsk. We are a little out of sorts this morning, aren't we? Obviously, you're not thinking clearly or you'd realize Kensington Gardens is where I followed our friend Victoria to."

"Give the information to Weymouth, then, and let *him* sort it out. As long as I know she's not in any danger, I've no intention of involving myself in Victoria's problems." Richard nudged the greys into a slow trot.

"Well, if that don't beat all. You set me to following the lady, and I spend I don't know how many hours—"

"I did *not* tell you to follow her. I merely asked you to keep an eye on her. And if she—"

"Hours of my time," Edward repeated reproachfully. "And now, when I've finally got a clue, you don't want to know. You may set me down. You may be faint-hearted, but I started this and I intend to follow it through."

Richard glanced at him, and felt the beginnings of a grin. The grin grew into a chuckle, and then an outright laugh as he saw the humour in the affair. Edward was looking offended, but was quickly mollified when Richard cracked the whip, calling out, "To Kensington Gardens, it is."

"Confess, Richard, you're as curious as I am to know who it is she's been meeting secretly."

"Not I. I only want to get to Yorkshire. I want to see the Abbey, and maybe figure a way to see Elizabeth. Do you know if she attends the assemblies in Harrogate?"

"More than likely, but we'll find that out when we arrive. Turn here," Edward directed, and looked back to make sure Kirby was following. "Victoria tried to give us the slip last night—changed carriages twice. But we were ready for her. I had Dawes follow her in one carriage, and when she slipped out, he followed the empty one. I was behind him, and I kept my eye on her. She hired a hackney to take her to the Gardens. I know the exact house."

"And what are we to do when we get there?"

Edward's expression of startled dismay was enough to set Richard laughing again, and he teased him unmercifully. "I can just picture it. We march up to the door, introduce ourselves and ask why Lady Weymouth is visiting the house secretly."

"I hadn't thought that far ahead," Edward owned sheepishly. "But we can at least spy out the place, try to find out who lives there. I wonder what a Bow Street Runner would do in such a case."

"Probably try to pass himself off as a census taker or some such."

"The very thing! We can say—"

"Edward, my friend, my dear friend, I hate to be the one to tell you this but...you look exactly what you are. Lord Edward Salford, son of the Duke of Cardiff. No one with an iota of sense would mistake you for anything else."

Edward looked down at his beautifully tailored coat of Bath Superfine, and owned Richard had a point. He beguiled the rest of the journey with proposing improbable solutions to their dilemma, including the suggestion that Roscoe be recruited to pose as a census taker, but was quick to retract the notion. Not that he didn't think Roscoe capable of the job, he assured Richard, but he'd a notion the Crown wouldn't hire foreigners to take the census. On that note they arrived in the Mews, and Edward was busy for the next few minutes locating the exact house.

Number six was a smallish house, and in much need of repair. A young girl, perhaps seven or eight, was playing on the stoop with her doll. She stared in amazement at such an elegant vehicle stopping in front and, leaving her doll, came closer for a better look. She appeared equally enthralled with the pair of greys as with the fine gentlemen driving. But the arrival of Kirby with the larger carriage sent her scurrying into the house.

Richard and Edward held a hurried conference with the others. They at last decided that Kirby should drive the carriage to the end of the street and wait there. They were attracting enough attention as it was with the curricle. Roscoe, who refused to leave in any event, was delegated to hold the horses while Edward and Richard paid an impromptu visit.

The plan, such as it was, was put in motion. Edward, agog with curiosity, and Richard, acutely embarrassed, approached the stoop. A curtain at the window twitched, and before they could reach the knocker, an older woman stepped out, pulling the door tightly shut behind her. Her hair, an unlikely shade of red, had no discernible style. She had a soiled wrapper pulled round her and bedraggled slippers on her feet. She glared at her visitors.

"If you're looking for a doxy, you've the wrong place. This here is a respectable house."

"I beg your pardon, ma'am," Richard apologized and tried the charm of his smile. "I *am* looking for a lady, but not that sort. I'm a friend of Lady Victoria Weymouth's. I know she's not here at present, but if I could perhaps leave her a message?"

Whether it was his smile or the mention of Victoria's name, the redhead looked less hostile. She regarded him more closely, listlessly scratching at her stomach all the while. "And just who might you be?"

"Richard Danvers, ma'am. I'm an old friend of Victoria's from India. Perhaps she's mentioned me?"

"That she has, sir, and I'm thinking you're just the one I need. I've been at wit's end, not knowing what to do, and no way to send a message to Lady Weymouth. Come in, come in. No sense in setting the neighbours to squawking."

She led the way, and once inside a dingy, scarcely furnished room, introduced herself as Mrs. Watson. Richard hastily introduced his friend as Mr. Salford, but he was of no interest to the woman, and after only a brief glance, she turned back to Richard.

"It's Harry, me 'usband, see? He's back and he don't 'old with me keeping the child. Wants 'er out of 'ere today. I was thinking of sending 'er and 'er abigail to a cheap hotel 'til Lady Weymouth comes back. But she wouldn't like it above half, and she's got the devil's own temper, she 'as. But 'arry's no better, and I got to live with 'im.''

"I see," Richard murmured, completely at a loss.

"'arry's a good man, but 'ard, you know? And he don't want no by-blow, uh...love-child in his 'ouse. Warned me to 'ave 'er out o' 'ere afore he gets back this day. You arriving just in time is a blessing. I'll send someone to fetch 'er, and you just take 'er with you.''

"Mrs. Watson," Richard cried as the woman started from the room, "wait. There's some misunderstanding. I can't take a child with me. Mr. Salford and I are leaving for Yorkshire this morning."

"All the better. I told 'er she were foolish ta 'ave the girl in London, just askin' for trouble. You take 'er along with you, and keep 'er 'id. I'll let Lady Weymouth know, don't you be worryin'.''

"Good Lord, woman, I can't take care of a child."

The redhead looked him up and down. "Guess Lady Weymouth was wrong 'bout you. I see 'ow it is. You can 'elp make a child, but can't be bothered with taking care o' 'er."

"Mrs. Watson, I never—"

"Get out of my 'ouse. Go on, get. I've no time for the likes of you. The child will be on the stoop in five minutes—with no place to go. If you don't take 'er, then it'll be on your 'ead, and so I'll tell Lady Weymouth." She picked up a broom and advanced towards him, brandishing it. Richard and Edward, with one accord, hurried outside.

CHAPTER ELEVEN

RICHARD, ANXIOUS TO PUT as much distance between London and himself as possible, would not agree to stopping at a posting house until they reached Kettering. Even then, he was reluctant to halt. Only after the curricle had hit a particularly deep rut, and Edward had castigated him as being four kinds of an idiot, did he own it was too dark to travel farther. At least, Richard consoled himself, they were still south of Leicester where most of the Quality would stop.

He drove his team into the yard of a very small inn, whose sign was hanging crookedly from its rusted chains. The hostelry, with its thatched roof and weather-beaten front, had little to recommend it from the outside. And even less when viewed by the light in the tiny parlour. Although neat and tidy, it contained only the one parlour, besides the common taproom, and three guest-chambers. Richard bespoke all three, the use of the parlour and supper for seven people.

The landlord, flustered in the presence of such elegant gentlemen, stammered and stuttered, and at last got out that there was not much to be had in the way of supper. "I . . . we ain't accustomed to entertaining the Quality, your honour. But if you was to condescend to a dish of ham and eggs, I'll have the missus serve you in an instant."

Richard was pleased to approve the ham and eggs, although Edward was inclined to be less generous and voiced his protests while the landlord bowed himself out to see to the bedchambers. He was interrupted as the little girl stumbled sleepily into the room, rubbing her eyes. She was followed by her abigail, Lucille, little more than a girl herself. Roscoe, Kirby and Dawes followed shortly, and it was a tired looking group which settled round the table.

"Are we racking up here, then?" Dawes asked Lord Edward, with an air of disdain for such contemptible surroundings.

Edward nodded, and sorted out the sleeping arrangements. "You, Kirby and Roscoe will share a room, the girl and her abigail another, and I'll bunk with Richard."

The valet nodded, resigned. Kirby and Roscoe shared a knowing look, but since neither had condescended to speak to Richard since he had persisted in his outlandish notion of taking up the girl, nothing was said. Dinner was tolerable, although quiet, with Lord Edward being the only one in spirits. He continued to view their bizarre cavalcade in the light of a lark and mocked Richard gleefully over Mrs. Watson's insinuation that he was the girl's father.

Richard knew Edward was not serious, and would've laughed off his jokes had he not been deeply concerned over the child. She was, he felt, unnaturally quiet, and she'd gone off with him without a word of protest. Been shuffled about too much, poor little mite. She had Victoria's long black curls, and large, dark eyes, heavily lashed. Her eyes were not those of a child, Richard fancied, but the eyes of a weary old woman who had seen the world and tired of all its follies.

He studied her as she finished eating. The girl ate everything placed before her without apparent enjoyment or complaint, and then sat quietly, hands folded in her lap.

"Violet, come here, please," Richard beckoned.

She arose at once and circled the table to stand before him, much as if she were awaiting judgement. She held her tiny back stiff and straight, kept her eyes downcast and clasped her hands demurely in front of her.

Richard placed a hand beneath her chin, gently raising her head. His hand trembled as he thought he saw a trace of fear in her eyes. He tried to keep his voice light and teasing. "I think it must've been dreadfully stuffy riding in a closed carriage all day. How would you like to ride in the curricle with me and Lord Edward tomorrow?"

Her eyes glanced to Edward and then back before she nodded her head shyly.

"Good. Now you run off and let Lucille put you to bed. We've a long drive tomorrow and you must get plenty of rest."

She nodded again, surprising him with a brief curtsey, before allowing Lucille to lead her from the room.

Edward took him to task as soon as they were alone that evening, warning that an apparent fondness for the little girl would be sure to be misconstrued.

"We've been over that ground a dozen times—you know it would've been impossible. The child's eight, and I didn't meet her mother until seven years ago."

"And that won't make a bit of difference to the gossips and tattle-mongers. You know they tend to add two and two and get four."

Richard grinned at him. "Two and two *are* four."

"You know what I mean. Before you can blink, it'll be all over Town that you're the chit's father. And Elizabeth won't like that, I can promise you."

"She'd like it even less were I unkind to the girl. Didn't you notice her sad eyes, Edward? Violet needs someone to show her a little kindness, and if the ton wishes to condemn me for that, then let them."

Edward gave it up, but Richard noticed that he was at pains the next day to amuse the child. She thawed a little under their gentle handling, and even volunteered a few remarks. When they stopped at a hostelry for luncheon, Violet disappeared for a few minutes. Richard found her outside feeding each of his greys an apple she'd cadged from the kitchen.

They reached Harrogate on Sunday afternoon. Violet was more at ease with them, and Richard let his thoughts turn to the Abbey. He almost dreaded seeing it, and knew the tightness in his stomach was from fear of what he would find. They passed through the town and turned west. The Abbey lay halfway between Harrogate and Skipton.

The first indication Richard had that something was amiss was the drive leading to the Abbey. He expected to find it badly rutted and overgrown. Not only was the road in excellent repair, but the lawns running beside it were neatly manicured before they gave way to the woods. Edward's attention was on the child, and Richard said nothing.

They rounded the curve from which the first view of the Abbey could be obtained, and Edward, chancing to look up, exclaimed, "You didn't tell me it was a bloody fortress, Richard!"

The original Abbey was founded in the twelfth century as a house for the Augustinian canons. That had long since been demolished, and a Carolean house was built around the courtyard with the plan of the Abbey. It had been remodeled during his grandfather's time and now boasted a Palladian west front, and three massive Ionic columns. Richard could not say a word. Weycross Abbey looked far better than he ever remembered it being. He whipped the horses, anxious now to see inside the house.

He brought the team to a neat stop in the wide, sweeping drive. Before they could alight, one of the monstrous doors opened, and an elderly man stared out at them. His face seemed to light up as he recognized Richard, and yelling to someone within the Great Hall, he hurried towards the curricle.

"Lord St. Symington, welcome home, sir. We've all been looking for your return any day these past seven years."

Edward stared at the old man who had obviously mistaken his friend for someone else, but Richard answered him calmly.

"Is that you, Clerihew? I'm surprised to find you still here, and even more amazed that you recognize me. I'm sorry to arrive without warning, but I scarcely expected to find the house staffed."

"No need to worry, sir. We've kept the house ready for you—and your guests as well," he added with a glance at Lord Edward and the child. "As for recognizing you, my lord, well you're the spitting image of your grandfather."

"I'm still astounded. We expected to camp out in the Great Hall. And the house—" Richard stood still, staring up at the huge edifice. "It's in wonderful condition, better than I remembered, in fact."

"Indeed, sir. Everything has been kept up just as you would wish, my lord. Now, if you'll just step inside, Mrs. Ponsonby will be eager to make you welcome."

Richard thought he must be dreaming, and mechanically followed the old man. Violet slipped her hand in his and trotted along beside him, but he did not notice. Edward, still puzzled by Richard's title and the size of the Abbey, trailed after them.

Mrs. Ponsonby, as promised, was waiting in the Great Hall. She seemed dwarfed by the immense room, for she was slight of inches and slender of build. Richard crossed to her side at once. Except for her gnarled hands, and the grey in her hair, she didn't appear to have changed much.

"I *must* be dreaming," Richard said, taking both her hands in his. "I only hope no one wakes me. Mrs. Ponsonby, how wonderful to see you again."

"My lord, we are pleased to bid you welcome home." Tears stood in her eyes as she looked up at him. Recollecting herself, she withdrew her hands and gestured towards Edward and Violet. "And you've brought guests. We haven't had guests at Weycross Abbey in a score of years."

"My wits are wandering," Richard apologized. "Lord Edward, may I present Mrs. Ponsonby. She was housekeeper here when I was a boy. I can't believe she's still here."

"I'm finding a number of things difficult to believe, *Lord St. Symington*," Edward returned, but with a sweet smile for the elderly woman.

Richard ignored him, pulling the young girl forward. "And this is Violet. She's the daughter of a friend of mine, and I'll trust you to take good care of her till her mother arrives. Her abigail should be along in a minute."

The commotion in the drive heralded Kirby's arrival, drawing the housekeeper and butler back to the door, and giving Richard an opportunity to speak quietly to Edward. "I know you've a thousand questions, and I'll do my best to explain everything if you'll grant me an hour or so. I must speak with Clerihew and find out what's going on here."

Clerihew, however, had not been of much help, as Richard explained to his friend later that evening. They sat in comfort in the library, which easily rivaled the duke's own in splendour. It was an unusual octagonal shape, with bookcases at least eight feet high lining all the walls. Above the books, a delicate wrought-iron railing circled the room, and the walls there were hung with some magnificent paintings. The gentlemen had elected to sit in the large wing chairs drawn up in front of the fireplace. The night air was still cool, and Mrs. Ponsonby had laid a fire.

Richard, sipping his brandy, looked round the room. Like the rest of the house, the library was in far better condition than Richard recalled from his boyhood. "All Clerihew could tell me was that a trust fund was set up to maintain the house and grounds after my father died. He always believed I was the one responsible for the trust."

"This goes beyond the realms of belief, Richard. It takes a vast amount of money to maintain a house of this size. How was the fund administered?"

"By solicitors. Clerihew was instructed to keep the house in readiness for my return, and to notify them of any item which stood in need of repair or restoration. He and Mrs. Ponsonby had the rooms restored one at a time, and it took the better part of three years. He said the solicitors had been most generous."

"An understatement, I would think."

"Assuredly. In addition to the butler and house-keeper, there are a half-dozen maids who come in daily, a cook, kitchen and scullery maids, and a battalion of gardeners."

"Is it possible that your father left the trust? Perhaps he had funds you knew nothing about."

"I considered that of course, but it's unlikely. One of the reasons I was sent to India was because of our financial problems. And every letter my father wrote spoke of his difficulties. Near the end, he even feared debtors' prison. He'd sold off all the land, excepting the few acres surrounding the house."

"If not your father, who then? Someone has gone to a great deal of trouble and expense on your behalf, my friend. The paintings and furnishings in this room alone must be worth a small fortune."

"As you said, the question is who? And why? Well, tomorrow I'll drive into York. The solicitors handling the fund have offices there, and surely they'll be able to tell me something."

"I'll go with you, if you like. I've the feeling that when you unravel this tangle, you may need a friend at hand."

Richard lifted his glass in salute. "Thank you, Edward. You *are* a good friend."

"But not good enough to trust with your true identity, Lord St. Symington," Edward said, still miffed at not being told before, although Richard had apologized. "I still don't understand why you felt it necessary to keep your title a secret."

"It seemed a good idea at the time," Richard said with a laugh. "I suppose I had some notion of learning more about father's affairs if no one knew who I was. Instead, it's only complicated matters."

"With Elizabeth, you mean? Promise me you won't tell Lady Fairchild until I'm present. When she finds out you've a fine old title to go with all that lovely blunt—Lord, I can't wait to see her face."

"That's all well and good, but it's the great-aunt I'm worried about. Were you able to speak with her before we left?"

"Only briefly," Edward said, frowning. "She was busy packing. In fact, she should be in Harrogate in a day or so to see Lizzie."

"Well, don't keep me in suspense. I can see by your long face you learned something. Let me know the worse."

"She's an eccentric, always has been, you know. I couldn't make sense of much she said, except that she remembered who it was you reminded her of. And wasn't at all pleased about it. Kept talking about bad blood. Bad blood will out, or some such nonsense."

"Perhaps it was my father," Richard owned, pain in his voice. "He had a problem with drinking and gambling. No worse than any of the other peers, of course, but he wasn't able to keep it in check very well. Clerihew told me he thought my father was going mad that last year. Turned him off without a pension, and Mrs. Ponsonby, too." He twirled the brandy in his glass, adding sadly, "There weren't any servants here when he died."

"I'm sorry, this must be hard for you."

"It's haunted me for years. I should have been here instead of living like bloody royalty in India. I could have helped him."

"Richard, you cannot blame yourself. Even had you been here, what could you have done? I've seen men addicted to drink. There's nothing anyone can do to help them."

"No. He only drank because he was driven to it, because he lost everything. Even his only son. He begged me to come home, you know. I can't help thinking that if I had been here, things would have been different. I might have been able to help him." He looked round the lavish room. "At least he would not have died all alone."

Edward didn't know what to say, but he hated seeing his friend so tortured. "There's no way of knowing what might have happened had you come home. The thing is to put it behind you. You have to think about what you can do now."

"Yes," Richard answered him curtly, his voice grown hard. "And the only thing I can do for him now is to make the man responsible for his downfall pay for it, and pay dearly. I swore I would do that."

LORD EDWARD Salford and Lord St. Symington were not kept waiting on Monday morning. The clerk, who admitted them to the inner offices of Bartlett, Boyce and Brennaman, disappeared briefly. He returned after only a moment to usher them into the offices of Sir Harold Bartlett, senior member of the firm of solicitors.

Sir Harold stood as they entered. He was a tall man, by any standards, with a lean build which indicated regular physical activity. Clear grey eyes spared only a glance for Edward, before studying Richard critically. He appeared to approve what he saw, and welcomed them both with a warm handshake and a gesture to be seated.

"Thank you, sir," Richard said. "I appreciate your seeing me so promptly without an appointment."

"But you've had a standing appointment with us any time this past seven years, Lord St. Symington. We've only been waiting your return from India."

"I might have been prompted to return sooner, sir, had I known. Did you never think to notify me?"

"You must hold me excused on that point, my lord. I have suggested we do so several times. However, I was specifically instructed to have no communication with you until you returned, voluntarily, to Weycross Abbey."

"If I might enquire, Sir Harold, who so instructed you?"

Sir Harold coughed, and made a pretext of shuffling papers on his desk. This manner of conducting business was not at all to his liking. He looked up to find Richard waiting. "I'm sorry, my lord, but I am not at liberty to divulge that information."

"I see. Perhaps you may tell me about the trust fund which was set up to maintain my home, then?"

"We may certainly discuss that. The trust was created approximately a month after the death of your father. It provides for the maintenance and upkeep of the Abbey and the lands surrounding it, as well as for the staff currently engaged. We were told to engage as many of the original staff as possible, and to pension them off when they wished to retire. Tenants were found for the farms and John DeFillby was engaged to oversee the estate management. The income from the farms, minus their expense, has been set aside in a separate trust for you." Bartlett smiled, adding, "It's quite a handsome sum now, my lord, and I venture to think you'll be pleased with DeFillby's efforts."

"What I wished to know is *who* set up the trust."

As if reciting by rote, Sir Harold repeated, "I'm sorry, my lord, but I am not at liberty to divulge that information."

Richard sighed in frustration. Sir Harold's manner told him clearly enough that he wished to be of more help. "My benefactor appears to have been extremely generous. Did he never give you any indication of why he should make such an extraordinary gesture?"

"To be quite honest, Lord St. Symington, I've often wondered why he insisted on remaining anonymous. All my client would say is that it is your rightful heritage."

"I take it then that your client is still among the living?"

"Indeed, yes, very much so. Although he did make stipulations in his will that should he die before you returned, the trust would continue. And that brings me to the next point. The trust is set up to expire exactly thirty days from the date of your arrival."

"Since I arrived yesterday, that gives me twenty-nine more days to enjoy his largesse," Richard said, rising. "You must thank my benefactor on my behalf, and tell him that I would very much like to do so in person."

"I shall, of course," Sir Harold agreed, "but I doubt it will do any good. My client has been peculiarly insistent on remaining anonymous. However, I am instructed to provide whatever assistance you might require in taking the reins in your own hands, so to speak. When you are ready, my lord, we can go over all the details."

"THIS IS A STRANGE TURN-UP," Edward said, once outside the offices. "What now?"

"Are you up to a drive to Harrogate? I might regain a semblance of reality if I could see Elizabeth. Right now I feel as if I'm in some dream world."

"Richard, have you truly no idea who your benefactor might be? Perhaps it's someone you did a tremendous favour for in the past? Or someone whose life you saved?"

"The only one whose life I ever saved, and that is still open to debate, is you, my friend. And I trust you won't feel compelled to go to such extravagant lengths to repay me."

"Not by half, even if I had the blunt," Edward assured him. "All you get is my eternal gratitude. I know—you're a bastard, Richard!"

"Thank you so much, my lord. Is it your notion of eternal gratitude to go round insulting your friends?"

"I only meant, suppose you were illegitimate? And your real father is a wealthy man who feels he cheated you out of your rightful heritage by not marrying your mother. This is his way of making it up to you, and, of course, he doesn't want it known because the scandal would ruin him."

Richard laughed aloud, but Edward was undaunted. "It all makes sense, Richard. It would explain everything."

"Excepting that I look exactly like my grandfather. Clerihew showed me the portrait of him in the Long Gallery. I hate to disappoint you, Edward, but there is no doubt that I am a true St. Symington."

Owing to their early start, they reached Harrogate a little after one that afternoon. Edward suggested Richard visit the Pump Room and take out a subscription, and he, meanwhile, would drive over to Durham Hall and try to bring Lizzie back with him.

Richard entered the Pump Room hesitantly. It was the first such that he had seen, and he was unsure what he should do. He need not have worried. Mr. Bartholomew Digby-Jones saw him at once, and came mincing across the room as fast as his studded heels would carry him.

Richard, watching him, wondered if he should retreat before it was too late. Digby-Jones was only of medium height (even with the heels), and his slender build was emphasized with a waist cinched so tightly that Richard was certain he was wearing a corset. An elaborately tied stock, exaggerated shirt points and a collar starched so heavily that he could barely turn his head proclaimed the man a dandy of the first water.

That Bartholomew Digby-Jones believed himself to be of some little consequence was evident when he introduced himself with all the air of one conveying a vast favour. When Richard failed to look impressed, he added, "You must know that I am in complete charge of the Pump Room, the Assembly Rooms and the subscriptions."

"Forgive me, Mr. Jones—"

"Digby-Jones, sir. Hyphenated, you know."

"I beg your pardon. You must blame my lack of knowledge on a long absence from England. I've only just returned from India, and a friend advised I should take a subscription."

"I see. Your friend is?"

"Lord Edward Salford, the younger son of the—"

"The Duke of Cardiff. Of course. I am well acquainted with Lord Edward. A pity he did not come in with you, Mr.... ?"

"Lord St. Symington," Richard pronounced, not knowing what imp of devilment prompted him.

Digby-Jones underwent an abrupt transformation. Gone was the superiour, elegant dandy condescending to the newcomer. All conciliation now, he bowed and fawned and flattered until Richard thought he would go mad. He personally took Richard on a tour of the rooms, introducing him to every dowager present, and bemoaned the lack of suitable young ladies to present to him.

"However, I am certain that once word gets round that Lord St. Symington of Weycross Abbey has joined us, we shall see a pleasant increase in the number of young ladies. The Abbey is much admired in these parts, my lord."

Richard, desperate to escape the clutch of Digby-Jones, and anxious to get out from under the eye of several calculating dowagers, gleefully hailed Edward's arrival. He took abrupt leave of Digby-Jones and crossed the room before the man could move. Taking Edward by the arm, he was out the door before his friend could utter a word. Even his disappointment at not seeing Elizabeth paled beside his relief at exiting the Pump Room.

And then he saw her. She was standing beside the curricle, and looking every bit as lovely as he remembered her. His heart skipped a beat or two as she smiled at him.

"Elizabeth, I am so glad you came."

"Did you think I would not, Richard?" she quizzed, giving him her hand.

"Only that you might be unable to get away. Can we stroll, or perhaps go somewhere for tea and talk for a few minutes? I have so much to tell you."

But Richard was not to escape so easily. The door to the Pump Room opened, and Digby-Jones, moving faster than one would have believed possible on his studded heels, hailed him.

"My lord, you forgot your card. The schedule, Lord St. Symington. You forgot the schedule."

CHAPTER TWELVE

RICHARD, WHILE WISHING Digby-Jones at the devil, was too much of a gentleman to do more than stare coldly at the dandy and issue a curt thank-you. The tension among the trio was palpable, and finally seemed to penetrate even the highly powdered wig of Digby-Jones.

As soon as they were alone again, Richard turned to Elizabeth. She took her cousin's arm, murmuring, "It appears we've been deceived, Edward. Are you acquainted with this Lord St. Symington?"

"Elizabeth, give me a chance to explain," Richard pleaded. "I swear I never meant to deceive you."

"He had his reasons, my dear," Edward added.

She looked from Richard's hopeful face to Edward's encouraging one, and relented. "Let us have tea, then, and you may tell me...about Lord St. Symington. But mind, I must not be away above half an hour or Mama will grow suspicious."

The half hour flew by. Elizabeth was amazed at the tale of Richard's unknown benefactor, amused by poor Lord Weymouth's mishaps and disturbed that Lady Weymouth's daughter was even now at the Abbey.

"I didn't know what else to do with the child, Elizabeth. She's such a quiet girl, unnaturally so, and far too dignified for her years. I could not drive off and leave her standing on that stoop."

"Ever the knight-errant," she sighed. And although she quite loathed Victoria Weymouth, she was still compassionate enough to feel sorry for little Violet. "Edward, you must call for me tomorrow and drive me to the Abbey. I wish to see this child."

"And me?" Richard teased. "I do want to show you the Abbey."

"There is that. I confess I've admired the grounds for years. Oh, Richard, it's so hard to believe that you are St. Symington. Everything is working out splendidly."

"Does that mean I'm completely forgiven? Shall I call upon your mother?"

"No...no, not yet. Let me think about it for a while. We must approach her in just the right way."

"Well, if you hope to turn her up sweet," Edward interrupted, "you'd best be saying your goodbyes. It's going on three o'clock."

"Three! Good Lord! I'd no idea it was so late. Mother will put me through an inquisition. Richard, I must leave at once."

"Must you? There's so much more I have to tell you."

"Tomorrow, dear one." She smiled, giving him her hand. They stood holding hands, their eyes conveying unspoken messages, for an indecently long time. Edward coughed loudly, knocking against Richard's arm. He let her go then, but stood as though rooted, watching her walk away from him. She paused at the door and, looking back, sent him a sweet smile. When he could no longer see her, he sat down, oddly content, and proceeded to spoon half a cup of sugar into his tea.

Richard was besotted, no other word for it, as Edward informed him roundly several mornings later.

"Here you are knee-deep in problems which need solving, and you just sit there, your wits wandering and your head in the clouds."

"You've only to add that I'm walking on air to complete an improbable picture."

"What? Now dash it, Richard, if you aren't going to talk sense—"

"I think I've only just come to my senses. Edward, I never realized how wonderful life could be. Now, isn't it time for you to fetch Elizabeth?"

"No, it bloody well isn't, but I'll go anyway, and drive slow. Watching the cows chew their cud in the pasture will be more amusing than sitting here watching you do nothing."

Edward was right, and Richard knew it. There were things he should have been doing. Instead, it was Edward who had sent off a message for Lady Weymouth, and Edward who had arranged to hire a pony to amuse Violet, and Edward who went over the dinner menu with Mrs. Ponsonby. Richard grimaced. He'd certainly been lax; he resolved to do better.

He was still sitting in the library, however, when Edward returned and ushered Elizabeth in. All else was forgotten. She looked enchanting in a white sprig muslin, sprinkled with blue forget-me-nots. Her blond curls were pulled back and held with a matching blue ribbon, and he knew an impulse to tug the ribbon and free her curls. Edward's look of censure restrained him, and he was quick to point out that he was just heading for the courtyard.

"Kirby tells me Violet has progressed amazingly well on her pony, and she wants to put him through his tricks for us."

"Wonderful," Elizabeth agreed, and Edward thought privately that she would say *wonderful* in just that tone if Richard told her the moon was made of green cheese.

Violet saw them as they neared the courtyard and waved excitedly. She and Elizabeth had liked each other on sight, and Elizabeth was now "Aunt Lizzie." Richard and Edward leaned against the fence and watched while Elizabeth entered the courtyard to give Violet a hug.

"I never thought she'd take to Lady Weymouth's chit like that," Edward said.

"It only shows what a kind, loving heart she has."

"If love addles your brain until you talk like a milksop, I pray I'll be spared such a fate. Besotted, the pair of you."

"She'll be a wonderful mother to our children."

"To be sure, *if* you're ever allowed to marry. Don't mean to be a crepe-hanger old man, but you haven't done beans about winning over Lady Fairchild or the great-aunt. And if Aunt Amelia finds out I've been bringing Lizzie over here every day, there will be real trouble."

"You're right," Richard sighed. "It's just that the past few days have been idyllic. Once we announce our engagement, you know the sort of fuss which will be made."

Elizabeth returned to them with instructions to watch. "Violet's going to canter her pony round the ring."

They watched and then applauded madly as the girl, intent with concentration, circled the ring twice. She brought the pony to halt before them and grinned from her seat. Flushed, and basking in their approval, she looked like a different child than the waif Richard had rescued.

"Uncle Edward, will you ride with me? Please? Kirby said I could go out a little, if you'd go with me."

With a show of reluctance for Richard's benefit, Edward nodded. The truth was he enjoyed the chit's company. Engaging little imp. And certainly more amusing company than Lizzie and Richard.

Left alone, the couple turned their steps towards the gardens. At the south end was an inviting gazebo, shaded from the sun, and conveniently shielded from any prying eyes in the house. It was one of the improvements made during Richard's absence and they had discovered it together the first day Elizabeth had visited. And retreated to its privacy each day since.

"Richard, I'm afraid this must be my last visit for a while. Edward is supposed to be teaching me to drive, but Mama is tired of hearing that. She wants me to make morning calls with her, and I dare not refuse."

"I know, dearest. I should've faced your mother days ago."

"I do think you should soon, or Mama will likely be paying a call on you. She and Lady Ormsby."

"Why? Has she heard something?"

"Only that the extremely wealthy and handsome Lord St. Symington has returned to Weycross Abbey," Elizabeth said, laughing. "Digby-Jones has told everyone in Harrogate, I do believe. And Mrs. Poole and Lady Evesham are in high alt. They are lording it over everyone because they have actually met you."

"They have? I don't recall—"

"Richard, darling, they are the two dowagers you met in the Pump Room. Surely you remember Digby-Jones introducing you?"

"Not a bit. My thoughts were completely on you."

"Richard! Do stop looking at me like that. We must concentrate."

"I am trying. If you wouldn't wear such fetching gowns— Very well. If we aren't to be undone, I must call on your mother as soon as possible. I had hoped to settle my affairs first, but—"

"What else is there to settle, Richard? I know you expected to find the Abbey in ruins, but it's been restored perfectly. And you said DeFillby is doing an excellent job overseeing the estate."

"He is. It's the outlying lands which I want to reclaim. Father was forced to sell them off, and I've had my solicitors negotiating with the owner since I arrived in London. Unfortunately, he is proving rather difficult. I received a message yesterday from Bailey, my solicitor. He informed me that the man will only deal with Lord St. Symington, and that if I wish to reclaim the lands, I must present myself in person."

"That sounds somewhat unusual, but surely nothing which cannot be postponed. Can it not wait until after our situation is settled?"

"It could, I suppose, but I would much prefer to get it done with before we wed. Elizabeth, you are too good, too kind-hearted to have ever hated anyone. I don't know if you can understand what it's like. I've loathed and despised this man for almost a decade. He ruined my father's life and drove him to an early death. For seven years, I swore vengeance against him. It's the only thing I can do for my father, and the main reason I returned to England. I hate him with a passion—a passion which has ruled my life, at least until I met you. I want to be done with him, put all that behind me, before I wed you."

"I see," she said, a little unnerved by his intensity. "You are right in that I've never hated anyone. My own father died when I was twelve, and though I loved him dearly, there was no one to blame for his death. I suppose if there had been, I might have hated that person. I can, at least, understand a little. You must do what you feel you have to, Richard. Only, I—I pray it won't take too long."

"Not a minute longer than necessary, I promise you. I shall see Lord Pembroke as soon as it may be arranged."

"Pembroke?"

"Lord Rowland Pembroke. I am told he resides outside Skipton, so it should not—"

"Richard, there is something dreadfully wrong here. You must have the wrong peer. Rowland Pembroke is my godfather."

He stared at her in disbelief for a moment. "There is no mistake, Elizabeth. My father wrote to me too often for that."

"But Uncle Rowland would never behave so odiously. He is the kindest, most gentle, loving man. Richard, I cannot believe—"

He released her hand and stood up, the scar beneath his eye pale and pulsating. He took a few steps away, and then turned and faced her. "He resides in Skipton, and refuses to see anyone but his family and few old friends. Isn't that true?"

"Yes, but—"

"And do you know why he lives so quietly?"

"He . . . he does not care for Society and the—"

"He ran off with another man's wife, Elizabeth. Is that the act of a kind and loving man?"

"Richard, I beg you to listen. You don't understand..." Tears stood in her eyes for she recalled the old scandal now, and it was worse, far worse, than Richard imagined. Had he looked at her, he might have gentled his tone, but he wouldn't look. Richard was filled with rage. Pembroke had stolen everything from him and his father, and in his heart he was afraid. Deeply afraid that Pembroke might take this girl away, as well.

"Pembroke is a liar and a cheat," he declared, his voice hard and angry. "He stole everything from us, and we weren't the only ones. Lord Demeral told me he lost his entire fortune to Pembroke. Did you know that?"

She nodded miserably, and tried to speak. "He...he deserved it, Richard. Demeral—"

"I suppose you think my father deserved to lose everything, too? Because he drank more than he should have and gambled foolishly, everyone condemned him. But a real gentleman wouldn't have taken advantage—wouldn't have driven him to his death. And that's what Rowland Pembroke did to my father."

"Richard, it wasn't like that. Uncle Rowland would never—"

"You're blinded, Elizabeth, like the rest of them—my old nurse, and Lady Sewell. Even my own mother. Pembroke has somehow managed to deceive you all. I shall have to see the old reprobate for myself. See what charms he has that blinds women to his true nature."

She stood then, trembling, with tears running down her cheeks. "It is you who are blind, Richard. Blind and deaf, too. And if you do anything, anything at all, to hurt my godfather, I will never forgive you."

She swept past him before he could move, and stumbled on the steps of the gazebo. Edward, just rounding the path in search of them, saw her and caught her in time.

"Careful there, Lizzie, do you want to break your neck?"

"Edward, take me home," she sobbed. "At once."

Startled, he looked up to where Richard stood watching them. He stood immobile, fists clenched and eyes blazing. Edward had never seen him look so furious, and promptly decided it was not a good time to ask what had occurred. With Lizzie crying on his coat, he tried to convey a helpless shrug to Richard before escorting her from the garden.

Richard stood where he was and watched her walk away, the sound of her cries tormenting him. She was walking out of his life and he wanted nothing more than to go after her. His arms already ached with the desire to hold her, and the empty feeling inside him threatened to overwhelm him. He sat down on the stone steps, resting his head on his arms.

He had a choice. Lord, how the gods must be laughing. Finally, he had a chance to do the one thing his father had asked of him. One small thing to atone for the years of neglect, for not coming home, for not being there when he died. One thing to absolve his own guilt. And if he took that step, he would lose Elizabeth because she would not forgive him. Not loyal little Elizabeth.

He didn't want to choose between Elizabeth and his sworn promise to his father. Why couldn't she understand? He *owed* his father. If only he had come home sooner, if only he'd been with him when he had died. But he hadn't. He had let his father down, left him to die penniless and all alone, with no one to mourn him.

"Your father was a wicked man." Chilly's words came unbidden to mind bringing Richard to his feet. He tried to deny her words with every ounce of his will, but deep within his heart he knew there was a vestige of truth. An onrush of childhood memories assailed him as he paced the gazebo. Memories he had kept locked away. Memories of his father as he really had been and not as Richard so desperately wished him to be.

He leaned against the stone parapet, his eyes wet with tears as he finally faced the bitter truth. He was the son of a man who was addicted to drink. A man who beat his wife, and who had gambled away his heritage. Once, in sheer frustration, Richard slammed his fist into the wall. The pain was a welcome companion and he scarcely noticed his bruised and bleeding knuckles.

Richard remained in the gazebo, tormented by his thoughts, and did not return to the house until late that evening. He found Edward waiting for him in the library, with the fire laid, and the brandy decanter set out. Edward, who had already made deep inroads into the brandy, looked up at his entrance.

"Been waiting for you. Thought you could use a drink. My father always told me that the course of true love never did run smooth, but a quantity of good brandy helps to ease the way."

Richard stretched out in the wing chair beside him, accepting the glass offered. "I thought it was Will Shakespeare who penned those lines."

Edward considered. "No, it was my father. Remember it distinctly. Says a lot of clever things, my father does."

"I believe *my* father's favourite adage was 'eat, drink and be merry.' He certainly drank enough," Richard said, and then added sadly, "but I don't believe he was ever merry."

The door opened and Clerihew entered, bearing a large tray. Without a word he crossed the room, sat the tray on the table between the gentlemen, and then silently withdrew.

Edward, who had eschewed dinner, looked at the tray with some interest. Large slices of thick, crusty bread, slabs of cheese, ham and beef looked very inviting. With studied concentration, he piled together two very large sandwiches, and passed one across to Richard.

"Good man you have there. Thinks of everything. Got to feed the inner man, you know."

"Is that something else your father said?"

"No, I think I said that. Father always said that man can't live by bread alone. Makes sense. Need something with it—ham, or cheese. Your man knows that."

Good man that he was, Clerihew checked on them a few hours later. He noted the tray was empty, as was the brandy decanter. Both of the gentlemen were stretched out in their respective chairs, snoring soundly. With a sigh, he helped Lord Edward up to his bed, and then returned to assist Richard.

He stirred slightly when Clerihew pulled him up, and managed to stagger along, one arm round the butler's shoulders.

"Father, poor Father..." Richard muttered, only half awake.

ROSCOE WAS THERE to attend him the following morning, with a vile-tasting potion which the valet swore would cure Richard's aching head, and coffee to wash it down.

"Best drink it up, my lord, for you've a caller downstairs, and from the looks of her, she won't take kindly if you keep her waiting."

"A caller? Who?" Richard demanded, hoping against hope that it might be Elizabeth.

"Mrs. Horatia Davenport, and she said to tell you, she ain't leaving until she's seen you."

And she wouldn't, either, Richard thought. She would remain fixed in the drawing room till midnight, if necessary. Dressing as quickly as possible, he hurried downstairs. Clerihew had put her in the Blue Drawingroom, and Richard noted she had made herself quite comfortable, with a tea service on the table by her chair.

"Good afternoon, Lord St. Symington," she said curtly, with a pointed glance at the clock on the mantel.

"Good afternoon, Mrs. Davenport. I gather Elizabeth told you of my title?"

"Elizabeth told me nothing," she snapped. "I don't need a chit of a girl just out of the schoolroom to tell me what's plain as the nose on my face. I knew who you were before Elizabeth left London. I knew both your grandfather and your father."

"I see. I don't know quite how to answer you, but I do apologize for deceiving you, even if my efforts weren't successful."

"Fiddle-faddle. Just tell me why you did it, and sit down, St. Symington, before you give me a crick in my neck. You look like you spent the night on the rack."

He obliged her by taking the chair opposite, and without thinking accepted the cup of tea she poured for him. "You knew my father, you said. Perhaps you also knew, then, that he was heavily in debt?"

She nodded. "Everyone knew. It would've been a wonder if he weren't. He drank to excess, and gambled prodigiously."

Richard's jaw clenched, and the scar beneath his eye pulsated rapidly at her frankness.

"Ha! That gets to you, doesn't it?"

"Whatever else he may have been, the man was still my father, Mrs. Davenport."

"Balderdash. That man was never a father to you, boy. He spent no more time at the Abbey than he had to, and when he was at home, he existed in a drunken stupor. If you wish to be defensive over your family, do it on behalf of your mother, who at least deserves it. He drove her half-mad with his excesses. He beat her, did you know that?"

Richard rose, his temper barely in check, and crossed to the door.

"Going to throw me out, are you?" the old woman chuckled. "Can't bear to hear the truth?"

"It is not a subject I wish to discuss."

"It's high time you did. A little plain speaking would have saved us all a lot of botheration." She paused, glancing round the room. "I haven't been inside these walls since you were five or six. On that occasion, your father was unchivalrous enough to slap your mother in front of me, and I vowed never to cross the threshold here again. I even tried to get Anne to leave with me."

Richard froze. A scene from his childhood came vividly to mind. Voices raised in anger, an old woman leaving in high dudgeon, and his mother running from the room, her hand held to her face. And there was a man there—a man threatening his father.

"Do you remember it, Richard? You were only a little boy at the time, and terribly frightened. I remember your

nurse got you out of the room as quickly as possible.''
Her voice was softer now, almost gentle.

Richard shook his head, almost dazed, and came to
stand in front of her. "Who was with you? Was there
another man here?''

"You do remember, don't you? It was Rowland Pembroke, and I had all I could do to stop him from calling
your father out. Perhaps I did you a disservice by stopping him. But it would have ruined him, and your
mother, too." She chortled then, her own rude self once
more. "Should have let him, they were ruined in the end,
after all.''

Richard sank into the chair, utterly weary. "Were
Pembroke and my mother..."

"Lovers? No, though he loved her right enough. Your
father thought they were, however. Of course, he thought
every man that looked at her was having an affair with
her. He never understood Anne's faith. She was Catho-
lic and deeply religious. She had taken vows with him,
before God, and she kept those vows, even if he broke
his.''

"I can remember her praying in the chapel.''

"That was her only comfort, boy. Her prayers. And in
the end, they did her little enough good.''

"Why are you telling me all this? Did Elizabeth send
you?''

Horatia Davenport stood, drawing her shawl about her
frail shoulders and gathering up her reticule. "No, Lizzie
didn't send me. But I saw her when she came home yesterday, poor miserable girl. She told me what happened,
and I couldn't sit idly by while you break her heart. Not
on behalf of a scoundrel like Andrew St. Symington. I
wouldn't give him the satisfaction.''

"For what it's worth, ma'am, I decided last night to...to put my quest for vengeance aside." It was the first time he spoke the words aloud and the agony in his voice was reflected in his eyes. "I was wrong...wrong about so many things. But there is one thing I don't understand. Edward told me you were against our marriage. You thought I came from bad blood."

"So I did," she snapped. "When I saw you in the garden with Lizzie, and realized you were Andrew's son, I almost had a spasm. Elizabeth is very dear to me, and I'd not allow her to end up like your mother. And if you were anything like Andrew St. Symington, I'd still be against it, no matter how much Elizabeth has her heart set on you. But you've a lot of your grandfather in you, and James St. Symington was as fine a man as ever lived. He asked me to marry him once, you know."

"What happened...at the end? With my mother and Lord Pembroke? You said they were both ruined."

"Pembroke will have to tell you that, boy. If he chooses."

"I intended to see him tomorrow. Would you tell Elizabeth I'd like her to go with me?"

"Tell her yourself. I'll be back tomorrow, St. Symington, and I'll bring Lizzie with me, and that whey-faced niece of mine, as well. See that you're up."

CHAPTER THIRTEEN

WHEN CLERIHEW OPENED the library door at eleven the next morning, Richard was certain it was to announce Mrs. Davenport. It was, however, a very different lady who brushed past Clerihew.

Victoria Weymouth, her hair in wild disarray, her travelling dress sadly dusty, rushed in without a thought to appearances or convention. Wild of eye, she demanded, "Where is she? Where's my daughter? What have you done with Violet?"

Richard rose at once and, crossing the room to her, took both her hands in his. "Victoria, calm yourself. Violet is perfectly fine. She's in the courtyard with Edward, practicing on her pony."

She looked near to fainting with relief, and Richard led her to a chair, instructing Clerihew to bring some sherry. She looked up, "I'm sorry, Richard. I should have known she'd be safe with you, but Salford's note—"

"I asked him to send a message to you as soon as we arrived, to assure you would *not* worry. What on earth did he say?"

Victoria gave him a weak smile. "It was most cryptic, I promise you. Something to the effect that the *package* I'd left in Kensington Gardens had been mislaid, and he had recovered it. If I wished to reclaim it, he said, I could do so at my convenience. Both he and the package would be at Weycross Abbey. I know I must appear foolish, but it seemed somehow ominous when I first read it.''

"I fear I'm to blame for your distress, Victoria. I asked Edward to send you a *discreet* note, in case it fell into the wrong hands. I should have written you myself.''

"It doesn't matter, as long as Violet is all right. I've been so worried. I left Weymouth a note and travelled all night in a hired carriage. If anything had happened to her, I'd never forgive myself.''

"I can understand that. Although why you left her with a harridan like that Watson woman—''

"Harridan? She seemed perfectly respectable to me. And I certainly paid her well enough to keep Violet. But how did you find her in the first place? I thought I'd been very clever in covering my tracks. And what possessed you to bring her here?''

"It was Edward." Richard grinned. "I believe he fancies himself some sort of detective. He was sure you were up to something and has followed you for weeks. He was behind you when you went to Mrs. Watson's Thursday night, and convinced me to return there with him on Friday.''

"How dared he! He had no right to interfere—''

"It is fortunate he did. I rather believe you owe him a debt of gratitude, Victoria. When we arrived, Mrs. Watson was on the point of putting Violet and her abigail out. It seems her husband returned home, and didn't wish to have your... uh, daughter in the house.''

"You may say it, Richard. My base-born daughter, my love child, or by-blow. I promise you, I know all the terms.''

"Victoria, if I hesitated it is only because we are all rather fond of Violet. She's a charming girl, no matter what her birth. Edward fairly dotes on her.''

"Salford?" she stared at him, disbelieving.

"She calls him *Uncle Edward.*"

"Does he realize?"

"Of course. She looks much like you, and it doesn't take a great deal of intelligence to make the connection. Victoria, why don't you tell Weymouth the truth about her?"

"He'd pitch me out, Richard, and then how would I support her? I've considered it, believe me, but Weymouth could cast me off without a pound, if he chose to, and then what?"

"Is that why you went to such lengths to obtain my assistance?"

She nodded. "I've been at wit's end to know what to do. I should've given her up at birth, but I could not. It's rather a common story, I suppose. I fell in love when I was seventeen. He was a soldier, and I met him while he was on leave. We planned to be married as soon as he could obtain leave again, but...he fell...fighting on the Peninsula. Violet is all I had left of him. I stayed with a friend of my mother's who understood, and she helped me to find a family to board Violet."

She paused, trying to regain her composure, and Richard handed her a glass of sherry. After a moment, she continued, "I visited her whenever possible, but when Weymouth said we'd be in London for several months, I advertised for someone in Town to keep her. Mrs. Watson answered the advertisement, and she seemed like a good woman, Richard. I knew it would be risky, the way Weymouth watches me, but I could not bear to be apart from my daughter for so long."

"He was convinced you were having an affair with someone, and I and Edward were at the top of his list."

"I am sorry, Richard. I truly never meant to cause you so much trouble, but when I saw you again...I thought I could convince you to return to India with me. You would have, once, and thought the world well lost. But if that didn't work, I knew I could at least obtain your aid."

"And the bruise you showed me?"

"A theatrical patch," she confessed, lowering her eyes. "My dresser got it from a friend of hers who is on the stage. You were so cold to me, and I was desperate, Richard. I thought if I could gain your sympathy...I did it for Violet's sake."

"You might have tried telling me the truth, Victoria."

That brought her head up, and her voice was challenging. "And if I had? Can you honestly say that you would have helped me?"

"I don't know. I probably would've advised you to tell Weymouth the truth—which is what I still advise. I think you do your husband an injustice. He paid me a call last week, and although I know you believe otherwise, both Edward and I were convinced the man loves you quite dearly. You could at least give him a chance to accept Violet."

"I can't risk it, Richard. He's not like you. He has so much pride, and to him appearances are everything."

"He's your husband, and you owe him the truth. Give him a chance, Victoria. I believe he may surprise you, but if I'm wrong, I swear I'll support you and Violet myself."

She smiled at that. "I suspect Miss Fairchild might have something to say on that head."

"Aunt Lizzie, do you mean? That's what Violet calls her."

Victoria could not credit what she was hearing, but promised him she'd think about it. At present, all she wished was to see her daughter. Richard showed her the way to the courtyard, and they stood together for a moment at the door, watching Violet and Edward. The younger son of the haughty Duke of Cardiff was kneeling in the dirt, oblivious of his trousers and shining Hessians.

"What does he think he's doing?" Victoria said, laughing.

"He's a notion that they can teach that pony of hers to shake hands. Go on out and see if they've had any success."

Richard returned to the library, thankful the great-aunt hadn't appeared while Victoria was with him. He could trust Edward to keep her out of the way for the rest of the morning. His relief, however, was short-lived as Clerihew opened the library door and was again pushed out of the way.

"You'll not fob me off this time, Danvers. I know my wife is here, and I demand to see her at once."

"Lord Weymouth," Richard acknowledged, rising. "I should, of course, have expected you. Please come in. That will be all, Clerihew, thank you."

"You admit she's here, then," Weymouth said, losing some of his bluster in the face of Richard's calm.

"Yes, Victoria's here. She arrived, as you must be aware, only a few minutes ago. You will see her directly, but first—"

"I'll see her now, and be damned to you. I'll not be cuckolded by you or any other man."

"Please lower your voice, Lord Weymouth. There is no need—"

"No need! Why you brass-faced young—"

"Lady Fairchild, Mrs. Davenport and Miss Fairchild," Clerihew pronounced loudly from the door of the library.

Damnation, Richard thought, and sent a look of silent appeal to Elizabeth as she entered with her mother and aunt. The warmth of her smile told him he was completely forgiven.

Amelia Fairchild took one look at Richard and shrilled loudly, "What are *you* doing here? Where is Lord St. Symington? Elizabeth, I warned you I'll not countenance—"

"And who invited you in here, my lady?" Weymouth interrupted, turning his livid gaze on her. "I'll thank you to leave. I've private business with Danvers here."

Edward chose that moment to walk in with Victoria on his arm, and Violet clinging to his hand.

"Clerihew told me Weymouth had arrived, and I'd thought you might stand in need of reinforcements." His voice was grave enough as he glanced round the room, but he had a look of devilment about him which made Richard distinctly uneasy.

Mrs. Davenport's voice rose above the chaos. "You'll have to wait, Weymouth. We've an appointment with him." She pointed her bony finger at Richard, and he swore there was a look of unholy mirth in her eyes.

"I won't wait—I was here first. And I want a word with you, too, Salford. Unhand my wife."

"Certainly, my lord. And if you'd care to step outside, I should be delighted to teach you not to jump to conclusions."

"Not with *him*, Aunt." Amelia was gesturing wildly. "You're confused. That's Richard Danvers."

"Richard Danvers St. Symington," Horatia chuckled, her strident voice raising above the rest.

Silence fell for a moment, and into the silence came Clerihew's deep voice, "The Duke and Duchess of Cardiff."

The duke stood in the door, his dark eyes surveying the room, and giving away nothing of what he felt. Her Grace stood beside him, regal in her bearing, but plainly agitated. She did not miss noting Victoria's hand resting on her son's arm, or the child standing beside him, who bore a striking resemblance to that young woman.

Confusion reigned for some minutes as everyone attempted to speak to the duke at once, with the exception of Richard. He stood wishing he could escape with Elizabeth to the gazebo. It was a tempting thought, but she was trying to calm her mother. Edward and Weymouth were engaged in a shouting match, while Victoria tried to explain her sudden flight to the duchess, who was not listening at all complacently, and the great-aunt was encouraging them all, while Violet stood silently next to Edward, her eyes round with amazement.

Seeing that there would be little chance of sorting matters out until the various parties were separated, Richard stepped forward and spoke loudly enough to gain the attention of all his visitors.

"Your Grace, I'm honoured by your visit, but I think your first wish must be to speak with your son alone. If you would be so kind, my butler will show you and Her Grace to the Blue Saloon, where you may talk in private." Edward, in answer to his silent plea, and somewhat embarrassed, crossed the room to his parents and urged them to follow Clerihew.

"Lord Weymouth," Richard continued more quietly, "I think it would be wiser to postpone our discussion until you've had a chance to speak with your wife. I assure you I shall be available if you still wish to call me out. Violet, be a good girl and show them the drawing-room next door. And then run up and let Lucille give you lunch."

Violet went at once to the door and stood waiting patiently. Victoria was a realist. Believing she had nothing left to lose, she took Weymouth's arm. He stared at the child, and then back at Victoria, bereft of words. His wife smiled at him, and with promises to explain everything, led him out of the room.

Elizabeth had settled her mother on the sofa beneath the windows and found the smelling salts in her reticule. Amelia, while still pale, had regained enough of her spirits to demand an explanation. Horatia, settled in one of the wing chairs by the fire, was chuckling hoarsely.

Elizabeth rose gracefully and stood next to Richard. "Mother, we had not meant to break this to you so suddenly, but Richard Danvers *is* Lord St. Symington."

"I don't understand. If *he's* St. Symington, why didn't he say so in London? Why would he want to go round masquerading as a commoner?" She reached for the smelling salts. "Has the world gone mad?"

"Lady Fairchild, I'd not been in England since I was ten, and I was not certain when I arrived if I would stay here or return to India. I didn't know what kind of reception I would receive if I appeared as St. Symington. And I have since learned that my father was, I regret to say, not the gentleman I believed him to be. Under the circumstances—"

"Andrew St. Symington was a black sheep, there is no question as to that. The best of families have them. But the St. Symingtons are a fine line, one of our oldest families, and King George thought very highly of your grandfather. Why, I'm told he even visited here once. And Weycross Abbey..." She glanced round at the elegant room. How anyone could own such magnificence and not boast of it left the poor lady speechless.

"Thank you, Lady Fairchild. I am, of course, using my title now, and I've decided to remain in England. I hope to do what I can to...restore the St. Symington name."

"Now that is more sensible. And, of course, the first thing you must do is begin entertaining. I shall assist you in any way possible, but it is most unfortunate that you do not have a hostess," she said, looking about her with a covetous glance.

"I am delighted you feel that way, Lady Fairchild, especially since I wish to wed Elizabeth. Perhaps this is not the time to discuss it, but the duke has said I might tell you that we have his blessing."

"Oh, my dear boy. Nothing could please me more." Tears stood in her eyes as she rose and hugged first Richard, and then Elizabeth. This was the sort of marriage she'd envisaged for her daughter, and she conveniently forgot all her animosity towards Richard.

"Lady St. Symington of Weycross Abbey. It is all a mother could hope for. And Elizabeth, my dearest, you'll be close enough that I can drive over frequently, for I'm certain you'll stand in need of my advice in running this great house."

"Yes, Mother," Elizabeth smiled, exchanging a wry glance with Richard.

"And now that Lord Pembroke has—"

"Mother," Elizabeth interrupted, "why don't you have Clerihew show you about the Abbey? Richard and I should see the duke and duchess." Clerihew was summoned and Amelia went off with him quite happily. Richard cast a questioning glance at Horatia.

"Not me, dear boy. I shall just sit here and enjoy the sherry, and perhaps see what other miracles you produce."

Richard paused outside the door and kissed Elizabeth soundly. "I think I quite deserve that."

"Indeed, sir, you handled Mother wonderfully. Before the day is over she'll come to believe our marriage was her plan from the beginning."

He could not resist kissing her once again. "Now, who do we see to first? Weymouth or the duke?"

"The duke, of course. He quite outranks Weymouth."

It sounded peaceful enough, Richard thought, as he stood outside the door of the Blue Saloon. But then, one wouldn't expect either the Duke or Duchess of Cardiff to stoop to the vulgarity of raised voices. He tapped lightly on the door before entering.

"St. Symington, come in," the duke welcomed him, and spared a warm look for Elizabeth. "Edward has just been telling us something of what the pair of you have been doing."

"I regret that if anything we've done has caused you or Her Grace distress. You must have been gravely concerned to have abandoned your guests and journeyed here."

"A slight misunderstanding—no more than that," the duke said, honouring Richard with one of his rare smiles. "Lady Weymouth was careless in leaving behind the note which my son sent her."

"Ah, yes, that note. It also brought Lady Weymouth here, with her lord in hot pursuit," Richard said, sending Edward a dagger glance.

"You said to be discreet," Edward protested. "How was I to know she'd leave it lying about for the whole world to read?"

"You're quite right, Edward," the duke told him, surprising everyone. "However, I believe your taste for trailing people about and sending cryptic messages could be put to better use in the Home Office."

"Do you mean it, sir? I promise I'd not let you down."

"Both your mother and I feel the idea has some merit. We'll discuss it more fully, Edward, but for now I suggest we let our host see to his other guests."

"Thank you, Your Grace," Richard said, drawing Elizabeth to the door. "And I'd be honoured if you both could stay with us for some days?"

"Delighted to, St. Symington. I shall expect to drink a toast to you and Elizabeth before we leave."

"Two down, one to go," Richard said, taking a deep breath outside the drawing room.

"It's terribly quiet in there, Richard. Do you suppose he's strangled her at last?"

Richard tapped gently and then opened the door. Victoria and her husband hastily broke what appeared to be a passionate embrace. Victoria blushed, and Weymouth stepped forward to extend a hand to Richard, though he still kept one arm possessively round his wife.

"Vicky said I owe you an apology, my lord, and I can't say as how I disagree. I might have said a few harsh words before I, er, understood the situation. But I know as how you're not one to bear a grudge, so what say we let bygones be bygones?"

"Done, sir," Richard said, taking his hand while he smothered a laugh, thinking of Weymouth's notion of a few harsh words.

Victoria smiled and added, "You'll be pleased to know that William has suggested he legally adopt Violet. She will make her home with us from now on."

"Oh, I'm so glad," Elizabeth said, reaching out a hand to Victoria. "She's a charming girl. And you must promise to bring her to visit often."

"That might be difficult, Miss Fairchild. We've decided to return to Calcutta."

Weymouth nodded. "Now that they're going to open up the trade, there should be some interesting opportunities for a man who knows a thing or two."

"We must talk later, sir. I'm inclined to sell my holdings there, if you think you might be interested."

"Capital. I can see I'm going to need all the advantages I can get with two ladies to take care of. It was bad enough with just Vicky, but now I've got Violet to think of. Going to be a looker, too. Just like her mama," Weymouth boasted.

"And a very lucky little girl to have such a doting papa," Victoria said, looking at her husband with such gratitude that Elizabeth and Richard felt decidedly *de trop*.

Richard spoke for both of them. "I hope you will excuse us. Elizabeth and I have a prior engagement, but we shall return in time for dinner. When you are ready, Clerihew will show you to your rooms, and please ask him for anything you require."

Richard doubted that they heard him as he quietly shut the door. "That turned out rather better than I hoped. I expected Weymouth to ride roughshod over her for a bit."

"If Victoria had an affair while they were married, it would have been a disaster. But I fancy since it was before she met him, Weymouth will accept it with good grace. He really does dote on her," Elizabeth said, smiling up at him.

"Odd, I always thought the Abbey such a large house, and suddenly it seems immensely crowded."

"And such an odd assortment for a house party," she teased.

Lady Fairchild rounded the corner of the hall with a harassed-looking Clerihew in tow. "There you are, Richard, dear."

"Lady Fairchild, you are just the person I need. Could I possibly impose on you? Elizabeth and I must leave at once if we are to keep our engagement with Lord Pembroke, and I have only now realized we will set down ten to dinner this evening. Someone must advise the housekeeper, and decide on a menu—"

"Say no more, I am delighted to assist you, and you must know that I have always been thought to excel at small dinner parties. Clerihew will direct me to the kitchens."

Elizabeth watched her mother sweep down the hall behind Clerihew. "Richard, cry shame! We shall return to find your chef and your butler resigned their posts."

"I'll gladly wish them all at the devil for a few minutes alone with you. You will come with me to see Pembroke, won't you? At least, we shall have a little privacy during our drive. Come, let us make good our escape before your great-aunt decides to join us."

Laughing, Elizabeth allowed Richard to pull her through the Great Hall and out the massive doors. They found Kirby and Roscoe anxiously awaiting them. News of the betrothal had spread amazingly fast, and no one was more pleased than his two faithful retainers.

"We just wanted to wish you happy, my lord," Roscoe said, speaking for both of them. "Of course I knew

how it would be from the first when you came home telling me how Miss Fairchild—''

''Thank you, Roscoe,'' Richard interrupted hastily.
''Now if you will have my curricle brought out, Miss
Fairchild and I have an engagement with Lord Pem-
broke.''

''Well, sir, seeing as how you've Miss Fairchild with
you, and jest engaged and all, Kirby and me thought we'd
drive you in style. We got the old barouche out, and all
cleaned up for you.''

Richard grinned, knowing the pair had some notion of
protecting him if the meeting with Pembroke did not go
well. And recollecting that the heavy barouche, with the
crested door panels, would allow him far more privacy
with Elizabeth, gave his consent. He was, after all, enti-
tled to steal a few kisses.

CHAPTER FOURTEEN

THEY ARRIVED at Lord Pembroke's all too quickly to suit Richard. The light-hearted feeling he had enjoyed with Elizabeth in the cosy confines of the carriage vanished as he surveyed the domain of the man he had hated for so many years. The Manor House, modest for a man of Pembroke's reputed wealth, had an air of serenity about it which Richard found pleasing in spite of himself.

The last quarter-mile was accomplished in silence, with only the warmth of Elizabeth's hand to comfort him. He had given her his promise that he would deal civilly with her godfather, and he prayed he'd be able to keep his word. Although he realized that Pembroke was not the villain he'd imagined, it would still be difficult to face with equanimity the man his father had hated so immensely.

The carriage stopped, and Richard, more than a little uneasy, stepped down. He helped Elizabeth to alight, and was again thankful for the warmth of her hand in his as they approached the entrance. The door was answered promptly by the butler, and although he looked at Richard with frank curiosity, there was nothing in his manner to convey either approval or disapproval. He greeted Elizabeth warmly, expressing his pleasure at seeing her again.

"Thank you, Marston. Is Uncle Rowland expecting us?"

"Yes, miss, but he asked that you go directly to the Conservatory. Lord St. Symington will join you there later."

Richard made no objection. He, too, thought it would be better if he saw Elizabeth's godfather without her, but Elizabeth looked at him with concern.

"You've no need to worry, I promise," he said, trying to reassure her. But he felt oddly bereft as he watched her walk down the long hall away from him, leaving him alone with the butler.

The man led him up a flight of curving stairs and down a narrow hall to a room at the end. Richard had a fleeting impression of a feminine-looking room. Delicate wall hangings, soft blue and green colours and a profusion of plants reinforced the impression. Small tables were adorned with lace and silk cloths, and embroidered pillows were scattered on the various sofas.

The curtains were drawn against the afternoon sun, and it took Richard a minute to adjust his eyes to the dim light. At first, he thought the room empty. Then he saw the woman seated near the window, and he knew this must be her private sitting room. She gave no indication that she was even aware of his presence, but Richard had the feeling she was watching him closely.

"Lady Pembroke?" he ventured at a guess. "I apologize for disturbing you, ma'am. There appears to be some mistake. I have an appointment with Lord Pembroke, but your butler brought me up here."

"There is no mistake. I directed Marston to bring you to me. I've waited years to see you. Later, perhaps, you shall speak with my husband. Would you oblige me by coming near that I might see you better?"

The gentle voice was hauntingly familiar, and he was drawn by it without conscious thought. He stepped closer, and realized why the woman hadn't risen at his entrance. She was in a wheelchair.

No one had told him that Lady Pembroke was crippled, and he didn't know what to say. She, however, did not seem to feel the need for words, and simply sat staring up at him. Her hair, once blonde, was now a silvery grey which curled in soft waves across the wide brow. Her brown eyes were set beneath slightly arched brows, and fine lines were etched round them. Lines of grief, Richard suddenly thought, with no notion of why.

"You know then, that I am Richard St. Symington?" he asked, partly for the sake of something to say, and partly because he wished to hear her voice again.

"Yes, I know. I believe that I would know you anywhere."

"Did you know my grandfather, then? I am told I look a great deal like him," he asked, wondering what it was he'd heard in the low, melodious voice. Bitterness? Mockery?

"Yes, I knew him. I knew your father as well, much to my regret." She turned her head then towards the window, eyes downcast. There was a familiarity about the movement, about the way she held her head, about the silhouette of her against the curtain...He reached out blindly, kneeling before her.

"Mother?" It was a plea, as much as a question, and he held his breath, not daring to hope, not daring to believe.

"Richard, my son," she answered him, her hands trembling as she lovingly touched his face and smoothed the hair back from his brow.

For a long moment, they held each other, with no need for words. Richard's tears fell on her hands, while his hair grew damp with her own. When he could speak again, Richard looked up.

"I don't understand—Father wrote me that you had *died!* I still have the letter."

"I know. Josiah wrote me. Your father lied, Richard, as he lied about so many things, may God forgive him."

"But if you knew, why didn't you write me? How could you let me go on thinking you were dead?"

"Sit down, Richard, and we will talk," she said gently. "There are so many things I must tell you, so many things you don't know. Draw your chair closer." She waited till he was seated, and then reached out for his hand and held it tightly within her own.

"For years and years, I've thought of what I would say to you if I ever saw you again, and now that you are finally here, I don't know where to begin. The pleasure of seeing you has made me forget everything I planned to say."

"It doesn't matter, Mother. Now that I've found you again, I promise you that—"

"Don't make rash promises, my son," she told him with one of her tender smiles, which he recalled from so long ago. "I fear you have much to forgive me."

In answer he lifted her hand to his lips.

"I know you never really understood why I sent you away. It...it was one of the hardest things I ever did. And when you wouldn't answer my letters, I resigned myself to losing you altogether. I knew you hated me for what I'd done."

"No, I could never hate you. But I was deeply hurt. I thought you didn't love me, and I wanted to hurt you back. Not answering your letters was all I could do. It was stupid, of course, but I was only a boy. When I was older, I swear to you I regretted it. If I had only known you were alive—''

"I know," she soothed. "When I made the decision to send you away, it seemed to me to be the only thing I could do. Your father was a difficult man to live with. He was deeply troubled, Richard, and his slavery to drink was an affliction which we all paid the price for." She paused, taking a deep breath. "Your father used to beat me. Beat me badly. I never wanted you to know."

"I realize that now."

"I hoped you would never have to know, Richard. That's why I sent you to Josiah. I wanted to protect you, son," she said, her voice breaking slightly.

"I understand, Mother. I only wish I'd known sooner that you were alive. We've wasted so many years."

"I'm to blame for that, but I always thought... Although you would not write me, my brother did. I've always known what you were doing and how you were progressing. And I thought that when Andrew died, you would come home..."

"I wanted to, but Josiah talked me out of it. There was the business, and he wasn't in good health— Mother, why didn't Josiah ever tell me the truth?"

"We...we thought it was for the best, at least while Andrew was still living. I tried to do my duty by your father, Richard. I stayed with him for as long as I could bear it. Then, when you were twelve or thirteen, he came home from one of his trips unexpectedly. He was there when Rowland Pembroke called."

"He wrote me about that. He suspected you were having a love affair with Pembroke."

"I wasn't, at least not in the way your father believed. If I were ever unfaithful to him, it was only in my heart. Rowland was one of the few friends I had, and I came to love him, and to depend on him. He cared about me in a way Andrew never did. Your father somehow sensed that, and it infuriated him. That day... your father had been drinking more than usual. Rowland didn't know he had returned, and he called that afternoon, as was his habit, when Andrew was away.

"I had no chance to get word to him... Your father and I were in the upstairs sitting room when we heard Rowland arrive. He...he was angrier than I had ever seen him, and I was afraid of what he might do. When he rushed out to the landing, I followed him. I was frightened, and I suppose I had some idea of stopping him.

"I saw him—standing at the top of the stairs, trying to load a pistol. Rowland was in the hall below. When Andrew raised the gun, I threw myself against his arm. The shot went wild, and in his fury, Andrew shoved me. I don't...I don't believe it was intentional, but I fell down the stairs."

"Mother! I had no idea it was so bad. And remembering all this is distressing you. You don't have to say anything more."

"No, it's better you know the whole story now. Too much has been kept from you for too long. I don't know precisely what occurred, for I was unconscious. I know Rowland called Mrs. Ponsonby and Clerihew to attend to me, while he rode for the doctor. Mrs. Ponsonby told me later that Andrew locked himself in the library. I think he knew that Rowland would have called him out, if he interfered.

"Dr. Layton came at once. Do you remember him, Richard? He's a good man and a good doctor, but there wasn't a great deal he could do. He didn't want me moved, but Rowland insisted I be brought here, and it was he who faithfully nursed me. There was a tremendous scandal, of course. A married woman leaving her husband and living with another man. Poor Rowland was ostracized for his devotion to me.''

"You are the lady he ran off with?" Richard asked incredulously. "I heard in Town that Pembroke had run off with another man's wife, but I never dreamed that it was you."

"Oh, yes, the gossips made much of it. Most of them never even knew that I was crippled. Rowland...cursed them for their stupidity, and became a recluse here, with only me for company, and a few close friends who understood. Andrew was furious, but he also feared Rowland. I don't know what passed between them, but Andrew left us alone. His only means of revenge was through you. He wrote me a letter telling me that you believed me to be dead, and he threatened to tell you that I was an adulteress if I ever dared write to you."

"You should have written me the truth. I would have believed you."

"Would you?" she asked gently. "You hated me then, and I knew from Josiah that you thought your father had been badly treated. And there were many who condemned me for leaving Andrew."

His silence was her answer.

"Don't be concerned, Richard. You were only a boy, and I would not have burdened you with things the way they were. And I was not...unhappy. Rowland saw to everything for me. I had only to express a wish, for it to be done."

"Pembroke. And all these years I pictured him as some sort of villain. I only came to London to seek vengeance on him, did you know?"

"I suspected as much. There are some friends who have remained loyal, in spite of the scandal I created. Blanche Sewell wrote me after you called on her."

"She tried to tell me the truth, but I wouldn't listen. And Chilly, too. Did you know I paid her a visit? She told me about Father abusing you, and I'm afraid I didn't behave very well. I think I knew she spoke the truth, but I didn't want to admit it. Then yesterday, Horatia Davenport called." Richard laughed ruefully. "She spoke some home truths about my father which I had little choice but to accept."

"Knowing Horatia, I can well imagine. Richard, I realize it must have been difficult for you. I sometimes think that Andrew must have been insane. While he was writing you all those letters, he was deliberately destroying your estate. Because I cherished you, he wanted you to have nothing."

"Then he failed dismally. The Abbey is in wonderful condition, far better than I ever remember it being."

"Rowland saw to it for me. As Andrew sold off the acreage, Rowland bought it. And when your Father died, Rowland arranged for the restoration to begin. He even found Mrs. Ponsonby and Clerihew, and arranged for John DeFillby to oversee the estate until your return."

Richard shook his head. "I can't believe how blind I've been. I blamed him for all Father's troubles. When I arrived in London, I tried to find out what I could about...Lord Pembroke. I heard the gossip about him running off with another man's wife. And then there was a Lord Demeral who claims Pembroke cheated him out of his estate."

"I don't imagine Demeral saw fit to tell you that Rowland gave all his winnings to young Gerant's family—the young man Demeral drove to commit suicide."

Richard bowed his head. "No, no one said, though I doubt if I would have listened. I was ready to believe the worst of Pembroke. And he is the man I have to thank—not only for the Abbey, but for his care of you. I owe him a tremendous debt."

"He will accept your thanks, and gladly, Richard," she said, smiling. "I think he is a little afraid of meeting you."

"Afraid? Why, when I am so much in his debt?"

"Because he knows how very much I love you, and because Rowland has always felt partly to blame. Not only for my accident, but for the way Andrew treated you, too. Now if you will pull the bellcord, Marston will come. He carries me downstairs whenever I wish."

Richard crossed and pulled the bellcord, but it was he who proudly carried his mother down the stairs and through the long hall to the Conservatory. Elizabeth was there, anxiously waiting for him, and she said a silent prayer of thanksgiving as she saw the tender look on his face as he helped Anne to her chair.

When his mother was settled comfortably, Richard motioned Elizabeth to his side. "Mother, I would like to present Miss Elizabeth Fairchild to you."

Both of the ladies laughed, though not unkindly, and Elizabeth explained, "Richard, I've known Anne for years and years. In fact, I know her better than I do you." Giving Anne a hug, she added, "She's been like a second mother to me."

"And there is no one I would rather welcome as my daughter-in-law than Elizabeth," his mother said.

"Is there nothing you don't know about me?" Richard quizzed her.

"Far too much, I'm afraid. But you shall tell me everything in good time. For the present, there is someone I should like you to meet."

Rowland Pembroke, who had stood unobtrusively at the far end of the Conservatory, came forward hesitantly. He was not a handsome man, by any standards. More frequently, he was known for his kindliness. His friends, when searching for a descriptive word, were wont to say he had a kind face, or kind eyes, or kind manner. Rowland had often wished that he had more inches to his height, or broader shoulders or a physique which was not running to a wider and wider stomach. He particularly wished it as he faced Richard St. Symington.

Richard, for his part, knew no hesitation, and promptly extended his hand. "Lord Pembroke, it is an honour to meet you, sir."

"Rowland. Call me Rowland. After all, I'm your father-in-law now," he said, turning a beaming look on Anne, pleased beyond measure that her son would accept him.

IT WAS AN ILL-ASSORTED group which sat down to dinner at the Abbey that evening. Richard had urged his mother and Rowland to come back with them, but travelling was still difficult for Anne. She promised, however, that she would come to Weycross for the wedding. In spite of all the sad memories the Abbey held for her, Anne wanted her son to be married in his own chapel.

As far as the wedding was concerned, Richard's only wish was that it be soon. Amelia Fairchild had taken over the house and turned it upside down. Both Clerihew and Mrs. Ponsonby had a word with him about it. He looked down the table where Elizabeth was sitting beside the duchess, and shared a smile with her.

"Just as well you're getting leg-shackled," Edward whispered to him, "if you are going to go about with that besotted look on your face."

"Careful, my friend. I've a feeling it won't be long before you'll be feeling the same. It must be something in the air. Only look at the Weymouths there."

Edward looked and made a derisive noise.

Richard rose, lifting his glass, and waited for everyone's attention. "I'd like to propose a toast. To Elizabeth, who has done me the great honour of giving me her hand in marriage, and to those already married, and whom we hope to emulate in their happiness. The duke and duchess, Lord and Lady Weymouth, and my own mother and stepfather, Lord and Lady Pembroke."

"Dear Anne," Amelia murmured. "I shall have to drive over there and discuss the wedding plans with her. It will be pleasant to see Anne again, for it seems like ages since last we spoke."

Horatia laughed loudly. "It's been years. You cut the connection when Anne left the Abbey."

"Really, Aunt, there's no need to dredge that old story up. I'm sure everyone but you has forgotten it entirely."

"They'll recall it soon enough when Elizabeth's betrothal notice appears in the *Gazette*."

"And to *Lord St. Symington*. I hadn't thought of that. What a brouhaha that will cause when it's discovered that St. Symington is Danvers. Or rather that Danvers is actually St. Symington. People will be so confused. Richard, dear, when are you returning to Town?"

"I'm not, Amelia. At least not any time in the near future."

"But, Richard, it's the Season. Everyone will wish to meet you. What can you possibly be thinking of?"

"My mother, and the Abbey," he answered promptly. "There is much to do here, and, besides, Town life really holds little appeal for me."

"But think of Elizabeth. You owe it to her to—"

"He is thinking of me, Mother. You know I was never happy in London. Richard and I want to get married quietly and live peacefully here. We'll leave London, and all the ton, to you."

"Leave them be, Amelia," the duchess advised. "Not everyone is suited to the demands of life in Town. I confess I almost envy them and am most reluctant to return to London and a houseful of guests. When we are entertaining, I seldom have a moment free."

"Why don't you come to us, Amelia?" the duke asked quietly. "Once you've seen Elizabeth married off properly, your talents will have little scope in Yorkshire. This dinner is excellent, by the way, and I'm told you had the ordering of it."

The duchess added her persuasion to that of her husband, and Lady Fairchild blushed at their praise of her social talents. Richard blessed them both, and the ladies withdrew to discuss the matter, while the gentlemen enjoyed their brandy and cigars.

Edward immediately engaged his father in conversation, peppered with questions about his possible service to the Home Office, and Lord Weymouth took the opportunity to speak quietly to Richard, offering his apologies.

"I assure you, sir, no apologies are necessary. Had our positions been reversed, I don't doubt I would have acted in much the same manner. I'm only happy that you and Victoria have settled your problems."

"We have, thanks to you. Don't know what might have happened if you hadn't talked some sense to Vicky. Don't be denying it, now. She told me you advised her to tell me everything. And I'm grateful to you."

It was the duke who rescued him from Weymouth's embarrassing effusions, turning the talk to India. Weymouth was at once all business. Richard, with a sigh of relief, drew Edward aside.

"Will you stay until after the wedding?"

"Of course I shall. Who else would act as groomsman? Besides, someone must keep an eye on you," he said, grinning.

"The problem is, my dear friend, there have been entirely too many eyes watching me. I wonder if you might create a small diversion when we rejoin the ladies?"

"Nothing to it," Edward agreed. "Though why you're so anxious to be alone with Lizzie is beyond me. Time enough for that after the wedding, you know."

Richard allowed this comment to pass, suggesting they rejoin the ladies. Elizabeth would be returning home with her great-aunt and mother shortly, and he desperately wanted a few words with her alone first. Edward, good to his word, took the first opportunity to point out to Weymouth that young Violet had a remarkable talent for the spinet. He stood back, with a wink for Richard, as Weymouth persuaded the girl to play for the company. And while they were all engrossed in her performance, Elizabeth and Richard slipped out unnoticed.

The garden was a haven of quiet after the noise of the drawingroom, with only the sound of crickets chirping to disturb the silence, and honeysuckle, just beginning to flower, smelling sweetly in the dusky evening. The moon provided just enough light to see the path, and Richard directed their steps to the gazebo.

He took Elizabeth in his arms as naturally as he drew breath, and kissed her deeply before whispering softly in her hair, "Thank you. Because of you this has been the happiest day of my life."

Leaning back in his arms, she smiled. "I'll wager you didn't think so this morning in the library."

"Lord, no! Did you ever see such a circus? Victoria frantic over her child, and Weymouth breathing fire—"

"And Aunt Horatia egging them on. She said she hasn't enjoyed herself so much in years."

"She and Edward. No wonder he's her favourite nephew. They both have a rather perverse sense of humour."

"Well, it *was* funny. Poor Mother was so confused over your identity, and arguing with Weymouth over who had the most right to the library—and then the duchess, worried to death over Edward! I do hope we won't be such foolish parents, Richard."

"I fear it is part and parcel, dear one. Unless, of course, you're going to be one of those unnatural mothers who don't love their children?"

"Most unlikely, sir, when I already love the thought of having a child by you," she confided, blushing.

"Children," he corrected, kissing her softly.

"Children," she agreed, nestling in his arms. "Lots of children."

The stillness of the night was broken abruptly. "Elizabeth, where are you? Elizabeth?"

"And speaking of fond, foolish parents, my lord," Elizabeth said, reluctantly, "I believe that is my mother calling."

"I didn't hear a thing," Richard said, kissing her again.

And from a distance, a hoarse chuckle disturbed the crickets, and an old woman's voice floated to them, "Leave them be, Amelia. Leave them be."

my VALENTINE 1992

Celebrate the most romantic day of the year with
MY VALENTINE 1992—a sexy new collection of four
romantic stories written by our famous Temptation
authors:

> GINA WILKINS
> KRISTINE ROLOFSON
> JOANN ROSS
> VICKI LEWIS THOMPSON

My Valentine 1992—an exquisite escape into a romantic
and sensuous world.

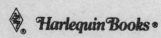

Harlequin Books ®

VAL-92-R

presents
MARCH MADNESS!

Come March, we're lining up four wonderful stories by four daz-
zling newcomers—and we guarantee you won't be disappointed!
From the stark beauty of Medieval Wales to marauding *bandidos* in
Chihuahua, Mexico, return to the days of enchantment and high
adventure with characters who will touch your heart.

LOOK FOR

      STEAL THE STARS (HH #115) by *Miranda Jarrett*
      THE BANDIT'S BRIDE (HH #116) by *Ana Seymour*
      ARABESQUE (HH #117) by *Kit Gardner*
      A WARRIOR'S HEART (HH #118) by *Margaret Moore*

So rev up for spring with a bit of March Madness . . . only from
Harlequin Historicals!

MM92

Take 4 bestselling love stories FREE

Plus get a FREE surprise gift!

HARLEQUIN
PROUDLY PRESENTS
A DAZZLING NEW CONCEPT IN ROMANCE FICTION

One small town—twelve terrific love stories

Welcome to Tyler, Wisconsin—a town full of people
you'll enjoy getting to know, memorable friends and
unforgettable lovers, and a long-buried secret that
lurks beneath its serene surface....

JOIN US FOR A YEAR IN THE LIFE OF TYLER

Each book set in Tyler is a self-contained love story;
together, the twelve novels stitch the fabric of a
community.

LOSE YOUR HEART TO TYLER!

The excitement begins in March 1992, with
WHIRLWIND, by Nancy Martin. When lively, brash
Liza Baron arrives home unexpectedly, she moves
into the old family lodge, where the silent and
mysterious Cliff Forrester has been living in seclusion
for years....

WATCH FOR ALL TWELVE BOOKS
OF THE TYLER SERIES
Available wherever Harlequin books are sold